BLUFF

Canyon O'Grady stared at
General Fernando Maximilan Fuljencio.
The Mexican was everything that Canyon
had heard—huge, brutally strong, his face
a mixture of animal appetite and
brilliant cunning.

Now that cunning glinted in Fuljencio's
eyes as he demanded, "You did not bring
the money, did you, gringo?"

"Did you bring the girl?" Canyon
countered.

"Of course I did," Fuljencio said.

Looking the man in the eye, Canyon
doubted that.

Then he was no longer looking the General
in the eye. He was looking into the barrel
of Fuljencio's gun.

"I want the money," Fuljencio said, "or I
will kill you where you stand."

Canyon swallowed hard. The game of liar's
poker was over. And his desperate
gamble against certain death had begun . . .

CANYON O'GRADY RIDES ON

CANYON O'GRADY

19

RIO GRANDE RANSOM

by

Jon Sharpe

A SIGNET BOOK

SIGNET
Published by the Penguin Group
Penguin Books USA Inc., 375 Hudson Street,
New York, New York 10014, U.S.A.
Penguin Books Ltd, 27 Wrights Lane,
London W8 5TZ, England
Penguin Books Australia Ltd, Ringwood,
Victoria, Australia
Penguin Books Canada Ltd, 10 Alcorn Avenue,
Toronto, Ontario, Canada M4V 3B2
Penguin Books (N.Z.) Ltd, 182–190 Wairau Road,
Auckland 10, New Zealand

Penguin Books Ltd, Registered Offices:
Harmondsworth, Middlesex, England

First published by Signet,
an imprint of New American Library,
a division of Penguin Books USA Inc.

First Printing, May, 1992
10 9 8 7 6 5 4 3 2 1

Canyon O'Grady

His was a heritage of blackguards and poets, fighters and lovers, men who could draw a pistol and bed a lass with the same ease.

Freedom was a cry seared into Canyon O'Grady, justice a banner of the heart.

With the great wave of those who fled to America, the new land of hope and heartbreak, solace and savagery, he came to ride the untamed wildness of the Old West.

With a smile or a six-gun, Canyon O'Grady became a name feared by some and welcomed by others, but remembered by all . . .

*Denver, 1858 . . . a place where
a man could find anything he wanted,
from women, to fortune,
to hired guns . . .*

1

The summons that brought Canyon O'Grady to Denver, Colorado, was an odd one. Considering that the message had come from Major General Rufus Wheeler—his superior—it should have carried the weight of an order and yet it did not. It was more like a request, which was enough to make the big redhead curious. Order *or* request, Wheeler knew that O'Grady would never ignore either one.

O'Grady arrived on Thursday, a day early, since he was to meet Wheeler in the Denver House hotel lobby on Friday, at noon.

O'Grady liked Denver, just as he enjoyed being in San Francisco. The cities were very much alike in that they each had much to offer. Both had theaters, museums—and lovely women. O'Grady always had the intention of meeting a lovely woman, but he did not expect the meeting to happen *that* evening at the theater—and especially not with a woman on the arm of another man.

O'Grady noticed the woman during the second act of the play. He would have noticed her earlier, but during the first act her escort had sat on the aisle, and she in the second seat. Now, for some reason, during the second act, *she* was seated on the aisle, across from O'Grady and down a few rows.

First he noticed her from the back. She had the

blackest hair he had ever seen, streaming down over creamy white, bare shoulders and back. When she turned her head to look at him, he noticed that she was extremely lovely, with full, red lips and dark eyebrows. She caught his eye, held it boldly, and then turned to watch the second act.

After the second act there was an intermission, during which the audience was invited into the theater's canteen for drinks. O'Grady rose and walked out ahead of the woman and her escort.

He was at the bar, getting himself a drink, when suddenly the woman was at his side. The scent of her perfume was not heavy, but it invaded his nostrils nevertheless, and he breathed it in with pleasure.

She was tall, about five ten, and the shoes she was wearing made her even taller.

"Are you avoiding me?" she asked. Her voice was low and husky.

"I don't even know you," O'Grady said, "but I would never avoid you."

"May I have a drink?"

He looked behind her and asked, "Where is your escort?"

She made a face and said, "He went outside to smoke a foul cigar."

Again, O'Grady looked around and saw men smoking in the room.

"I asked him to take it outside," she said. "The smoke bothers me."

"What would you like to drink?" he asked, when the waiter brought him his cognac.

"That's all right," she said, putting her hand on his glass, "I'll share yours."

She took his glass, sipped it, and passed it back. He didn't know how she managed *not* to leave a red mark where she drank.

"I lied, of course," she said.

"Of course," he said. "About what?"

"About why I sent him outside."

"I see."

"Do you?"

He studied her for a moment, then said, "I believe so."

"Can you meet me after the play?" she asked.

"Where?"

"Outside."

"And what about your . . . friend."

"I will . . . send him home."

"Won't that be awkward?"

"It might."

"There's another way, you know."

"Is there?" she asked. "What way is that?"

"We could leave now."

She looked at him through incredibly thick, black lashes and said, "But what about the play?"

"I've suddenly lost interest in the play."

She smiled and said, "So have I."

"There is a side door this way," he said. He had noticed it when he first entered. He always made sure he knew all the exits from any room he was in.

"Lead the way."

"Do you have a wrap?"

"They'll keep it for me," she said.

He put the drink down on the bar and said, "It's this way."

She was a slender woman, so slender that when he ran his hands over her sides he could feel her ribs. That made the size and weight of her breasts that much more of a surprise. They were round and full, with heavy undersides, wide, brown aureola and large nipples.

She sat astride him, the full length of him comfortably fitted inside of her. She leaned forward so he could run his mouth over her breasts, licking, biting and sucking her nipples as she rode him in a slow, rocking motion that made her catch her breath.

He slid his hands up over her ribs, around to her back and then down to her slender buttocks, where he held her, burying his face between her full breasts, still licking and biting.

Her hair was a wild, tangled mess that made her look like an untamed animal. The flaring of her nostrils added to the image, as well as the sleepy, yet fiery look in her dark eyes.

"Oooh, God, Canyon," she said, coming down on him hard, "you're . . . ooh, you're wonderful . . . I knew you would be as soon as I saw you in the theater . . ."

He didn't reply. His mouth was too busy, biting her, tasting her. Suddenly, her tempo increased and she began to bounce on him, up and down much more quickly. Her breasts were so firm they barely bounced, and since she was now moving about too violently for him to concentrate on them he closed his hands tightly over her buttocks and then succeeded in turning them completely over, without breaking contact, so that he was now on top.

"Oh, yes . . ." she breathed, arching her back as he drove into her, ". . . it's so . . . wonderful . . ."

He leaned down and licked the perspiration from her neck and shoulders as he continued to drive in and out of her, slowly at first, and then as violently as she obviously wanted it now.

"Oooh, harder . . ." she cried, "oh yes, oh God, I feel like I'm . . . going . . . to . . . explode . . ."

So did he, but he waited until *she* did, and then

allowed himself to go with her, that they both groaned aloud and soared together. . . .

"I saw you when we first entered the theater," she told him later, "but I couldn't see you during the first act, so I asked Conrad—that was my escort—to change seats with me. I told him I couldn't see over the head of the man in front of me. Then I was able to turn and look at you."

"I'm glad."

Her name was Linda Church. She was in her early thirties, and worried about it. He couldn't see any signs of age on her, but just from the things she said and did—she studied herself in the mirror before coming to bed with him—he knew that *she* did, but then *all* women saw an exaggerated onset of years in their chin, their neck, or the sag of their breasts. Her neck was smooth and beautiful, and her breasts sagged not at all. Because of their size, of course, they *would* sag eventually, but at this point he didn't see it.

"When did you see me?"

"When you changed seats."

"Not before?" she asked, contriving to sound disappointed.

"I'm sorry," he said. "I only arrived in Denver today, and I spent the day sightseeing. I was tired. Of course, I didn't see any sights all day long that were as beautiful as you are."

"Oh," she said, "you're sweet . . ."

He leaned over and licked her shoulder and said, "So are you."

"Lower," she said.

He licked the slopes of her breasts.

"Lower . . ."

He licked and bit her nipples.

She moaned aloud and said, "Oh Canyon, lower . . ."

He went lower . . . and lower . . . and lower, until his head was buried between her trim, smooth thighs. He licked the moist folds of her, then spread them and thrust his tongue into her. She arched her back and lifted her ass from the sheet as he found her clitoris, and then her hands were on his head, as if she were afraid that he would move, or try to get away. Of course, he made no such attempt, and *kept* licking her until she cried out and released his head to grasp the sheet tightly in her fists.

He rose over her and entered her then, riding her roughly, and she wrapped her legs around his waist and scraped his back with her nails until once again they both cried out together . . .

They were in his hotel room, so it was she who rose and dressed to leave.

"What will your escort say to you?" he asked.

"Oh, he'll complain," she said, "but I can handle him."

Dressed, she went to the mirror to do something with her face and her hair.

"I look a wreck," she said, turning for his approval when she was done.

"You look incredible."

She went to the bed, sat on it and kissed him, deeply, wetly, a long, searching kiss, and then she said again, "You're sweet."

"Do you have to go?" he asked. "There's plenty of time before daylight."

"I'm a creature of the night," she said. "I must get home before daylight."

"Will you tell me where you live?" he asked. "Or where to find you?"

"Oh, no, darling," she said, "I couldn't tell you that. It would ruin the mystery."

"What mystery?"

"Of whether or not we'll ever see each other again."

"We can solve that now if you'll tell me—"

"No, no," she said, "you don't understand. I don't *want* to solve it. I'm a spontaneous woman, darling. What I did tonight I did on the spur of the moment. You see, Conrad was not only my escort, he's my husband."

"I see," O'Grady said, although he wasn't altogether surprised. "And his name isn't Conrad."

"That's right."

"And yours isn't Linda Church."

"Well," she said, "it isn't Church."

"I see."

"I hope you do," she said, putting her hand on his face. "I hope you're not . . . disappointed, or offended."

"Neither," he said. He put his arm around her, drew her to him and kissed her as she had kissed him, a long, lingering kiss.

"My God . . ." she said, pushing him away breathlessly.

"Stay," he said.

"I can't," she said, rising, "but we'll meet again."

"When?" he asked as she went to the door. "Where?"

"I don't know the answer to either of those questions," she said, "but we'll meet again. I'm sure of it. I can *feel* it."

She blew him a kiss, opened the door just wide enough to slip through, and then left.

He lay there silently for a few moments, marveling at what had happened, and how it had happened, then turned over and tried to sleep on sheets that retained the smell of her, and of their sex.

2

O'Grady skipped breakfast, figuring that he and Wheeler would meet over lunch. Not that either of them wanted to have lunch with the other, but it was the most indiscreet way for two men to meet. Simply talking in the lobby might have attracted undue attention.

When he came down for the meeting he was thinking about Linda Church—or whatever her name was. When he awoke that morning her scent was still strong in the bed, and so was the memory of the things they had done together. It had been exciting, probably because of the unexpected way the whole thing had started. Maybe she was right about not planning another meeting. If and when they did meet again, he hoped that it would be as spontaneous—and as good. The fact that she was married did not seem to bother him at all, although he normally stayed away from married women.

This, however, was definitely not a normal situation.

When he saw Rufus Wheeler in the lobby of the hotel, all thoughts of Linda were pushed aside, and he became all business.

Wheeler looked uncomfortable away from Washington and out of uniform. He had a lost look on his face until he saw O'Grady. If the redhaired agent didn't know better, he would have thought Wheeler was relieved to see him.

"Rufus," O'Grady said as he approached the man.

Wheeler almost took O'Grady to task sharply for not using his rank when he realized that, where they were, the agent was *correct* in not using it.

"O'Grady," Wheeler said. "Where can we talk?"

"Why don't we have lunch," O'Grady suggested. "The food here is excellent."

Wheeler scowled, then said, "I *could* use a decent meal."

"This way . . . sir."

The "sir" seemed to make it up to Wheeler for having to forgo his rank for the meeting.

They were shown to their table by a waiter. The hotel did *not* employ waitresses.

They ordered their lunch, and Wheeler asked for a pot of coffee immediately.

"How was your trip?" O'Grady asked.

"Appalling," Wheeler said. "I'd rather not talk about it."

"I was just making small talk, anyway," O'Grady said. "We might as well get down to business."

"Yes," Wheeler said, "I think we should—although this does not really come under the heading of business."

"I beg your pardon?" O'Grady said.

"What I'm about to discuss with you is not really an assignment, O'Grady," Wheeler said, "it's more of a . . . favor."

"A favor to whom?"

"To the government."

"Sounds like an assignment to me . . . sir," O'Grady said.

"Well, it's not," Wheeler said, annoyed. "Take my word for it."

"Yes, sir," O'Grady said. Apparently, the favor Wheeler was about to ask for was something he would rather *not* be asking for. O'Grady decided to keep quiet and let his superior get to the point in his own time.

The waiter appeared with the coffee and took his time setting the cups down, filling them, and then asking if there was anything else he could get them.

"Just the lunch," Wheeler said.

"As soon as it is ready, sir," the waiter said, and walked off righteously.

"All right," Wheeler said, "let me get to it. We— the government—would like you to have dinner tonight with a man named Arthur Doyle."

"Okay," O'Grady said.

"Don't you want to know who is he?"

"I figure you're going to tell me."

Wheeler frowned. O'Grady was trying not to annoy the man, yet seemed to be doing so. On second thought, Wheeler had probably left Washington annoyed, arrived in Denver annoyed, and he'd probably leave the same way. O'Grady wondered if Wheeler personally knew Arthur Doyle.

"I will tell you," Wheeler said, "tomorrow at breakfast."

O'Grady frowned.

"Why tomorrow?"

"I—we—don't want you to listen to Doyle with any preconceived notions."

"About what?"

"About him!" Wheeler said. "Look, just come down here tonight at seven for dinner. He'll have a table in here already."

"How will I know him?"

"Don't worry," Wheeler said, "as I understand it,

everyone knows Mr. Doyle. You'll be shown to his table."

"And?"

"And you'll have dinner with him and listen to him," Wheeler said. "We'll talk again in the morning."

O'Grady couldn't resist.

"Will you be in a better mood in the morning?"

Wheeler glared at O'Grady and said, "I doubt it. Maybe tomorrow I'll tell you why."

The waiter came with lunch and set their plates in front of them. Beef for O'Grady, salmon for Wheeler.

"Maybe I'll be in a better mood after this," Wheeler said.

Silently, O'Grady hoped so.

After lunch Wheeler did seem somewhat mollified, even to the point of apologizing.

"I'm sorry to be biting your head off," he said, "but perhaps you'll understand it tomorrow."

"I hope so . . . sir."

"Look," Wheeler said, "just enjoy the rest of your day and be here for dinner at seven.

"After I listen to this Mr. Doyle, what am I to do? I mean, I'm assuming that I'm going to be asked to do something. Do I tell him yes or no, or do I wait to see you for that?"

"Make no decision until we speak again," Wheeler said. "Sleep on what you hear from the man and we'll talk in the morning."

"How long will you be in town, sir?"

"No longer than necessary," Wheeler said. "I'll be catching a train tomorrow afternoon."

"Uh, would you like some more coffee?"

"No," Wheeler said, then added grudgingly, "thank you." He stood up and said, "I have a room at an-

19

other, less ostentatious hotel. I'm going to go there and get some rest. I'll see you in the morning."

"All right, sir," O'Grady said.

"Why don't you stay and have some dessert?"

"I think I will."

O'Grady watched Wheeler leave the dining room, then called the waiter over to order dessert. He was listening to the waiter tell him what the chef's dessert specialties were when there was a shot. Not everyone in the dining room looked up, but O'Grady did.

"Oh, my . . ." the waiter said.

O'Grady got up and rushed out into the lobby.

"Where'd that come from?" he asked the desk clerk.

"Out front, I think, sir," the clerk said. "Shall I send someone for the police?"

"I think you better," O'Grady said.

He rushed to the front door and when he went outside saw that a crowd had gathered not far from the hotel entrance.

"Shit," he said, and moved towards the crowd. He elbowed his way through, muttering "Excuse me's" along the way, and when he finally broke through he saw a man lying on the street, facedown. There was a hole in his back, oozing red.

"Damn it," he muttered, and leaned over the man because no one else was doing anything more than looking. He turned the man over and, somehow, was not surprised to see the face of Rufus Wheeler.

"I knew it."

Wheeler was alive, and had been removed to the nearest hospital. O'Grady was sitting in the lobby, waiting for the police to get to him after they talked to "witnesses" from the street. O'Grady was still undecided how to play it with the police. Obviously he couldn't claim not to know Wheeler because they had been seen having lunch together. By the same token, he couldn't tell the police who he and Wheeler were. The United States' Secret Service was just that—secret. O'Grady couldn't reveal their existence—or his and Wheeler's identities—without first checking with the proper authorities. Unfortunately, under normal circumstances Rufus Wheeler would be that someone.

O'Grady saw a man approaching him, and the man definitely had an official bearing, as if he were used to people rising when he came into the room. O'Grady rose and waited for the man to reach him.

"Thank you for waiting, sir," the man said. "I am Inspector Lawrence Names, of the Denver Police Department. And you are . . . ?"

"Inspector," O'Grady said, sticking out his hand. Names hesitated just a moment before taking it. He was in his late forties, a man who carried a lot of weight on a not-too-tall frame. He had a brush mustache which hid his upper lip, and short cut brown hair. His height was hard to gauge, due to the weight, but O'Grady guessed him at about five ten.

"My name is O'Grady, Canyon O'Grady."

"Mr. O'Grady," Names said, nodding. "Are you a guest in the hotel, sir?"

"I am."

"Do you know the gentleman who was shot?"

"I do," O'Grady said.

"And what is his name?"

"I don't know."

"Sir?" Names said. "I don't understand. I thought you said you knew him."

"I do—sort of. Actually, we met yesterday at the theater, and agreed to meet here for lunch today. To be quite truthful," O'Grady said, laughing as if it were the silliest thing in the world, "I've managed to forget his name."

"You've forgotten his name?" Names asked. "Sir, the man has been shot, and anything you can tell us would be very helpful. How could you forget—"

"I know, I know," O'Grady said, "believe me, it was very embarrassing. All through lunch I was trying to recall his name, and it just wouldn't come to me."

"I see," Names said. "You haven't just forgotten his name since he was shot."

"Oh no," O'Grady said, "goodness, no. It just slipped my mind since last night, and I haven't been able to—I'm truly sorry about this, Inspector. I know his name would be of great value to you."

"Yes," Names said, studying O'Grady. "Well, the man is still alive. If he remains that way, we will be able to get his name from him . . . won't we?"

"I guess so," O'Grady said.

"Do you know what the man did for a living?"

O'Grady shook his head and raised his hands helplessly.

"I'm afraid not."

"Excuse me, Mr. O'Grady," Names said, "I'm having a difficult time understanding this. You met the man last night at the theater—er, presumably spent some time with him then—and *then* you had lunch with him today, and you never once asked him what he did for a living?"

"That's right," O'Grady said, "and neither did he offer."

"Mr. O'Grady," Inspector Names said, "what do *you* do for a living."

"I'm afraid this won't sound very good to you."

"Try me," Names said, finally beginning to show his irritation and impatience.

"I'm a gambler."

"Ah," Names said, as if that explained a lot.

"Inspector, I can remember a winning hand I had a year ago, or the face of a woman I was with long ago, but I'm afraid names . . . are just not easy for me to retain." He hoped that the man wouldn't think he was trying to be funny with the comment about "names."

"I see," the inspector said.

"Of course, if I can recall something I will communicate it to you immediately."

"I would appreciate that," Names said. "Uh, did the man say anything at lunch that might lead you to think that he was, um, afraid for his life?"

"I'm afraid not, Inspector," O'Grady said. "We really just talked about the theater, and museums and—well, you know, the things men talk about . . . women . . . you know . . ."

O'Grady's tone was meant to imply that Names was a man and *he* knew what men talked about, but Names either didn't, or he was being deliberately obtuse.

"I'm sorry, Mr. O'Grady," Names said, "but if I spent that much time with a man, I'm sure I would remember his name, and what he did for a living."

"He never *told* me what he did for a living."

"So you said."

"And you're a policeman, Inspector," O'Grady said. "You're *trained* to remember things."

"Yes," Names said, "I am. Mr. O'Grady, you are familiar to me."

"Am I?" O'Grady said. "Have we met before?"

"I don't know," Names said, then allowed himself a smile which didn't touch his cold brown eyes at all. "You see, sir, even a policeman might forget a name, or a face."

"If you recall," O'Grady said, "I'd really like to know if we *have* ever met before."

"Oh, don't worry, Mr. O'Grady," Inspector Names said, "I'll be *sure* to tell you."

The policeman turned to walk away, then turned back and said, "Uh, you're not planning to leave town any time soon, are you?"

"I really don't know, Inspector," O'Grady said. "I usually make that kind of decision on the spur of the moment."

"Well," Names said, "just this once, think it over, all right? Let me know if you plan to leave?"

"Yes, sir," O'Grady said, "I'll be sure to do that."

"We'll talk again, Mr. O'Grady."

"Yes . . . sir . . ." O'Grady said. He was trying to appear—well, sort of helpless when it came to talking to the police. He knew that his appearance would belie that attempt, but it was all he could think to do.

Names stared at O'Grady for another moment or two, then nodded, turned and walked away.

"Oh, Inspector."

The man turned and said, "Yes?"

O'Grady had to phrase this carefully.

"Would it be all right if I, uh, went to see the man in the hospital?"

"If you like," Names said, with a shrug. "I don't see why not." The look on the man's face said that he wasn't so casual about his reply. He was wondering why O'Grady would want to visit a man he had just met in the hospital.

"I mean . . . he may not know anyone else in town," O'Grady said. "He might need the moral support . . . don't you think?"

"That's very . . . considerate of you, Mr. O'Grady," Names said. "Tell me, is he a stranger here?"

"Oh yes," O'Grady said, "that I remember. He's from . . . well, I don't know where he's from, but I do know that he's from out of town."

"Thank you for that little bit of information, Mr. O'Grady," Names said, unable to mask his sarcasm. "Yes, you may go and see him."

"At what hospital?"

"Holy Name Hospital," the inspector said, and his look *dared* O'Grady to make a comment about that.

O'Grady wouldn't have *dared*.

O'Grady's problem now was, if Wheeler died, who was he to notify in Washington. His dealings were usually with Wheeler and no one else. In the past he *had* dealt directly with the President. He supposed, if the worst happened, he could get a message to the President, although *that* certainly wouldn't be easy.

Before he made a decision like that, though, he'd have to go to the hospital and find out what kind of shape Wheeler was in.

If he knew his boss, he was too ornery to be killed by a single bullet.

3

When O'Grady arrived at the Holy Name Catholic Hospital, he presented himself at the front desk. There were two nuns in white habits there, one young and one old. The young one, her face devoid of any artificial coloring, was very pretty. The older one, however, was the one who turned to face O'Grady.

"Can I help you, sir?"

"Yes," O'Grady said, "there was a man brought in today, the victim of a gunshot wound."

"What is his name?"

"I don't know his name. In fact, I don't think even you know his name. He was shot in front of the Denver House Hotel."

"Oh, yes," the sister said, "yes, I know who you mean. Are you—no, of course you're not a relative, or you would know his name, wouldn't you?"

"I'm . . . I guess you'd say I was a friend, sister."

"And you don't know his name?"

O'Grady smiled disarmingly and tried to explain.

"Sister, I'm a stranger in Denver, so is he. We met last night and had lunch today, but we didn't really get to know each other, but there is no one *else* in town who will come and ask about him—except maybe the police."

"I see."

"I'd just like to find out how he is, and let him know that someone cares."

She studied O'Grady's face for a few moments, then said, "That's very admirable, sir, *very* admirable—don't you think so, Sister Marie?"

The older nun turned to the younger one, who had been listening.

"Yes, Sister Madrid, yes, I do."

"Can you tell me what his condition is, Sister?" O'Grady asked.

"I'm afraid the man is still in surgery, sir," the nun said.

"Can I sit and wait?"

Sister Madrid smiled and said, "Of course you can, young man. I'll let you know as soon as your . . . your friend is out of surgery."

"Thank you, Sister."

"Nonsense," she said. "Such . . . such consideration for your fellow man should be commended."

O'Grady smiled uncomfortably and said, "Uh, thank you, Sister—"

"May I get you a cup of coffee, sir?" the young nun, Sister Marie, asked.

"Why, yes, Sister," O'Grady said, "that would be fine. Just make it black."

"I'll be right back."

When she smiled she became even prettier. O'Grady found meeting and talking to a pretty nun somewhat disconcerting—given the thoughts he *usually* had when he met pretty young women.

He sat down and waited for his coffee and, ultimately, word on Wheeler's condition.

O'Grady was still sitting in the hospital lobby when Inspector Names came in.

"Anything on his condition?" Names asked O'Grady.

27

"I'm just sitting here waiting to hear, Inspector," O'Grady said. "I feel that somebody should."

Names studied O'Grady, obviously wondering if the man was for real, then turned and walked to the desk to talk to Sister Madrid. O'Grady could hear just enough to tell that she was giving him the same information about Wheeler's condition.

". . . need to question the man," he heard Names say.

"Inspector . . . some consideration . . ." Sister Madrid said.

". . . no time, Sister . . ."

". . . can't see him tonight . . ."

". . . soon as he's able . . ."

". . . let you know . . ."

Names turned away with a scowl on his face, then saw that O'Grady was watching him, and his face changed. He no longer showed any emotion at all.

"Good-day," he said, as he passed O'Grady.

"Good-day, Lieutenant."

O'Grady rose and walked to the desk. Sister Madrid saw him coming.

"Can I get you more coffee, sir?"

"My name is O'Grady, Sister," he said, "Canyon O'Grady, and no, the one cup was fine. Did the inspector give you a hard time?"

"An unpleasant man," she said, "but I suppose that is the nature of his business. No, he did not give me a hard time. I'm afraid I gave *him* one."

"Well," O'Grady said, "I don't think he'll charge you with anything."

"I should hope not!" she said, her tone serious, but then she smiled to show that she shared the joke.

O'Grady went back to his bench to sit and wait.

* * *

He was looking at his watch because he didn't want to miss his appointment with Arthur Doyle, when Sister Marie came over to him.

"Mr. O'Grady?"

He looked up and said, "Uh, Canyon, please, Sister."

"Canyon, then . . ." she said, with a small smile, "your friend is out of surgery."

"How is he?"

"He has survived," she said, "but they won't know anything for quite some time. You'd be better off coming back in the morning."

"When did the inspector say he'd be coming back?" O'Grady asked.

"Sister Madrid told him that we would notify him when the man could be talked to."

"I see," O'Grady said. "Thank you, Sister."

"You're very welcome."

She turned to leave and he called out on impulse, "Sister Marie?"

"Yes?"

"Do you know of a man named Arthur Doyle?"

"Why, yes, I do," she said.

"Who is he?"

"He's quite wealthy," she said, "and often appears in the newspapers—in the society columns, I'm afraid."

"Do you know what he does?"

"I'm afraid I don't," she said. "I do know that he donates a lot of money to charities. In fact, he has donated quite a bit of money to this facility."

"I see," he said. "Thank you, Sister."

Outside he looked at his watch again. He was surprised to find that it was five-thirty, five and a half hours since he had met Wheeler in the lobby, four and a half hours since Wheeler had been shot.

He had just enough time to get back to the hotel, bathe and dress to meet with the wealthy Mr. Arthur Doyle.

It was probably because O'Grady had found out that Doyle was wealthy that he decided to wear a suit to dinner. It was funny the way money affected people, and he was no different. Once, on his way down, he almost turned around to go back upstairs and change, but he decided against it. For one thing, to do so would have made him late, and he *very* much wanted to talk with Mr. Arthur Doyle. He wanted to find out if the shooting of Wheeler had anything to do with Doyle. Of course, it could have been coincidence, but O'Grady was not a firm believer in coincidence. Wheeler was in Denver to get *him* to talk to Doyle. What other reason could there be for someone to have tried to kill him?

He wondered if whoever had shot Wheeler would make a try for Arthur Doyle . . . or for him?

When he got to the restaurant, the maitre d' said, "Can I help you, sir?"

"Yes," O'Grady said, "I'm here to see Mr. Doyle."

"Of course, sir," the man said, almost coming to attention, "this way, please."

He followed the man across the dining floor to a large table near the rear of the room, where a man sat alone.

"Mr. Doyle," the man said with a small bow, "your guest has arrived."

Doyle stood up. He was only about five eight, with gray hair, a gray mustache and gray sideburns. He was wearing an expensive-looking three-piece suit, but it looked rumpled, as if he'd worn it since yesterday. O'Grady had a feeling that Doyle *always* looked that way. The man simply was not built to wear clothes well. Inspector Name's carried extra weight, but he wore his clothes well. Arthur Doyle, for all his wealth, was . . . well, dumpy was the only word O'Grady could think of, and dumpy men had trouble dressing.

"Are you from Rufus Wheeler?" Doyle asked.

O'Grady was very surprised to hear the name come from Doyle's mouth. He waited for the maitre d' to leave before replying.

"My name is O'Grady, Mr. Doyle," he said, "Canyon O'Grady. I've been asked to dine with you."

"Yes, indeed," Doyle said, shaking hands with O'Grady. "Please, be seated. Would you like a menu?"

"Under normal circumstances, I might, but since the meal is not the point of this meeting, why don't you just order for the both of us?"

"Very well."

Doyle raised his arm slightly and a waiter appeared at the table. Doyle placed two orders for a lamb dish, and dismissed the waiter.

"I suppose Rufus has explained—"

"Could we not use his name, Mr. Doyle?"

"Oh, yes, I'm sorry," Doyle said. "I'm aware that Ru—that he has a sensitive position with the government. I don't actually know what he does, but—"

"He was shot today."

Doyle fell silent and stared at O'Grady.

"I'm sorry," he said, finally, "but what did you say?"

"The man we're talking about was shot today, in front of this hotel."

"That's . . . that's terrible," Doyle said. He didn't show that much emotion at the news. "Er, is he . . . all right?"

"He's alive," O'Grady said, "but I don't know how long he'll remain that way."

"Where is he?"

"I'm not going to tell you that yet, sir," O'Grady said, shaking his head.

"Why not?" Doyle said. "Surely you don't think—see here, I could have my doctors look at him—"

Doyle had a point, but O'Grady wasn't ready to concede it—not just yet.

"Let's talk about that later, sir. I've been asked to listen to something you have to tell me. Could we get to that?"

"Do you think that . . . that my problem has something to do with Ru—with him being shot?" Doyle seemed genuinely shocked.

"I won't know that," O'Grady said, "until I know what your problem is, will I, sir?"

"Oh, please," Doyle said, waving a pudgy hand, "don't call me sir, Mr. O'Grady. If you insist on showing some kind of respect, just call me Mr. Doyle."

"That's fine, Mr. Doyle," O'Grady said. "Now could we get to it, please?" O'Grady was aware that he was showing more impatience than respect, but, dammit all, he *was* impatient. Finding out why Wheeler was shot started with finding out what Arthur Doyle wanted. He was almost sure of that.

"I really don't see what my problem would have to do with—"

"Please . . . Mr. Doyle?"

"Very well," Doyle said. "I will tell you what my problem is."

4

The story went like this: Arthur Doyle's daughter was staying with some friends on a ranch in South Texas, very near the Mexican border. It was a horse ranch, and Doyle's daughter, Anja—nineteen and "very pretty,"—loved horses. When she asked if she could go, her father said yes. The people who owned the ranch had known Anja since she was very little, and they were glad to have her.

It seemed that the ranch had been raided by Mexican bandits, who stole horses, killed a couple of ranch hands—and kidnapped Anja Doyle!

Later, it was discovered that these were not just bandidos, but soldiers of the revolutionary army of *Generalisimo* Fernando Maximilian Fuljencio.

O'Grady knew the name, but did not interrupt Doyle's story.

Apparently, the *generalisimo* knew who Anja was, knew that her father had a lot of money, and was now holding her for ransom. He wanted one million American dollars for the return of his daughter.

"I want to pay it," Doyle said.

"You have that kind of money?" O'Grady asked.

"And more," Doyle said, "but I'm not worried about the money. I want my daughter back, Mr. O'Grady, and I would like you to go in and get her."

"You want me to rescue her?"

"Jesus, no!" Doyle said, with his first real show of emotion. "That would endanger her life. I want you to pay the ransom and bring her back."

"I see."

"Will you do it?"

"Let me get this straight, Mr. Doyle. You didn't *ask* for me, did you?"

"I asked Ru—I asked our friend to send me the best man he knew for the job."

"Mr. Doyle, how do you know . . . our friend?"

"We've known each other for many years," Doyle said. "We went to school together, before I became a . . . a rich man, and before he became a . . . a soldier."

"I see."

"We're not really friends," Doyle said, "but I knew he was a soldier, with a high-ranking government position, and I am . . . a supporter of certain . . . politicians."

"Ah," O'Grady said. The word "politician" explained more to him than anything else Doyle had said up to that point.

"Will you do it?"

"I can't give you a decision now, Mr. Doyle."

"When, then?"

When, indeed? If Wheeler had still been available for their breakfast meeting, O'Grady could probably have promised Doyle an answer by the following afternoon or evening. Now, O'Grady didn't know if he'd *ever* be able to talk to Wheeler, and as it stood, he didn't know if he was supposed to do this as a favor to *Wheeler*, or to the United States government.

"I'm afraid I'll have to hold off until . . . our friend's condition has gone one way or another. When does the general want his money?"

"He gave me a month to raise the money, and to find a man who would be brave enough to deliver it," Doyle said. "We have three weeks left."

"How did the general notify you?"

"He had a message delivered to my friend's ranch, and my friend—his name is Charles Enright—sent me a telegram."

The name Enright was familiar to O'Grady, but he didn't have the time to dredge up the reason.

"Do you really think this has something to do with—with the shooting?"

"I can't see why it would," O'Grady said, honestly, "and yet I can't see how it could be anything else."

"Mr. O'Grady," Doyle said, "I beg you, don't endanger my daughter's life. I need an answer, and soon!"

O'Grady could appreciate Doyle's position. A decision *had* to be made. If O'Grady didn't go in and deliver the ransom, someone else would have to be found to do it. O'Grady knew of only one other man he would recommend—a man named Skye Fargo— but finding Fargo wouldn't be an easy proposition.

Wheeler had told him not to make any decisions, but Wheeler wasn't around now to tell him why.

"All right, Mr. Doyle," O'Grady said. "I'll do it."

"Bless you, sir."

"Do you have the money ready?"

"I can have it from my bank within an hour."

"Not this hour," O'Grady said. "We have three weeks, so I need about three days before I start."

"Three days!"

"I need the three days, Mr. Doyle, or I can't do it," O'Grady said. "Three days won't make much of a different, either way."

"No," Doyle said, "no, I suppose not."

He raised his arm, and a waiter appeared. Dinner

had been delivered while he was telling his story, but neither of them had touched their food. Now he asked the man for a piece of paper and a pencil, which the waiter produced immediately.

"This is my address," Doyle said, writing it down and handing the paper to O'Grady. For some reason, O'Grady noticed Doyle pocket the waiter's pencil. "Please, don't make me wait any longer than the three days."

"I won't," O'Grady promised. "I'll be in touch."

Doyle extended his hand across the table, and O'Grady took it.

"If . . . our friend sent you for the job, Mr. O'Grady, that's good enough for me. Thank you for agreeing."

"I'll do my best, Mr. Doyle."

"If you don't mind," the dumpy man said, "I won't be staying to eat."

"Oh, well, I can—"

"No, no," Doyle said, stopping O'Grady from rising, "stay and eat. The bill will be taken care of. Please, be my guest. It would be a shame for *all* of this food to go to waste."

"All right," O'Grady said, looking at the sumptuous meal that he had barely noticed earlier. "Thank you."

"I'll be waiting to hear from you."

O'Grady watched the man hurry from the room, moving with small, almost comic steps. He couldn't imagine Rufus Wheeler and Arthur Doyle as friends—and yet, Doyle had said they *weren't*. Surely, it was Doyle's money and political connection that had brought Wheeler to Denver—only to be shot down!

O'Grady thought for a moment that it might be inappropriate for him to eat, but then he realized there was little he could do for either Doyle *or* Wheeler right now.

He called the waiter over and asked, "Could I have a glass of wine, please?"

After dinner—and dessert—O'Grady left the dining room and started across the lobby for the stairs to his floor. As he passed the desk, the clerk called out to him urgently.

"Mr. O'Grady!"

He stopped and then approached the desk.

"Yes."

"A message came for you, sir," the man said, handing him a piece of paper.

"When?"

"Just about half an hour ago."

"Thank you." O'Grady was going to take it to his room to read, but decided to step off to one side and read it right away.

On the piece of paper was written:

O'GRADY

GET YOUR BUTT OVER TO THE HOSPITAL—NOW!
It was signed **RUFUS**.

It appeared that Wheeler was not only alive, but kicking, as well.

5

When O'Grady arrived at the hospital, it was almost nine P.M. Behind the desk, however, was the same older nun, Sister Madrid. With her was another nun of indeterminate age.

"Don't they let you go home, Sister?" he asked Sister Madrid.

She looked up from her desk and instantly recognized him.

"I'm afraid there is no rest for the . . . weary, Mr. O'Grady."

"Or the wicked, Sister."

"Well," she said, "I feel neither of us fall into that category, Mr. O'Grady. You're here to see your friend?"

"That's right."

"We were going to notify you—you *did* leave me the name of the hotel you were staying at—but he insisted on sending his own message."

"How is he, Sister?"

"He is terrorizing my sisters, Mr. O'Grady," she said. "He's doing quite well, according to the doctors—in fact, amazingly well."

"Can I see him now?"

"Under normal circumstances, visiting hours are over," she said, but then lowered her voice and said, "but I can get you in. I have pull with the man upstairs."

"I appreciate it, Sister." He also appreciated this woman's wonderful sense of humor.

"Sister, I'll be right back," she said to the other nun. To O'Grady she said, "Come this way."

He followed her down a long hall, then to the right and down another. Finally, they arrived at a closed door, and there was a policeman outside of it.

"I'm glad to see our friend Inspector Names is alert," he said aloud.

"Oh yes," she said, "the inspector was here and spoke to Mr. Wheeler—that's his name, Wheeler, by the way."

"Oh, that's right," O'Grady said, as if he'd forgotten and she had just reminded him.

She looked at him much the way Names had.

"He seems to feel there might be another attempt," she said.

When they reached the door, she said to the policeman, "This man is allowed to see the patient."

"Sister," the policeman said, "I can't let anyone—"

"Young man," she said, cutting him off—and he *was* very young—"I'm sure that on the street you are in complete authority, but you are in my battlefield now, and I am in charge. Do you understand?"

"Yes, Sister."

"Besides," she said, "the inspector knows this man, *and* the patient asked for him."

"Well . . . all right," the policeman said.

"You can go in, Mr. O'Grady—but you must make him be quiet."

"Thank you, Sister."

O'Grady entered, wondering if he should report the young policeman for allowing him to enter so easily.

From the bed, Wheeler saw him and exploded. He was lying on his right side, propped up by something behind him.

"Goddamn it, O'Grady," he said, "where the hell have you been."

"Actually," O'Grady said, "I spent most of the day here, but if you don't keep your voice down I'm going to get kicked out."

"Well, what the hell—" Wheeler started, then stopped and continued in a lower tone. "What the hell happened?"

"Didn't the police tell you?"

"There was an Inspector Names here, but he asked more questions than anything else. I want *you* to tell me what's going on."

"I don't know much . . ." O'Grady said, and went on to tell his superior was he *did* know.

"So we have no idea who fired the damned shot?" Wheeler said.

"No, sir," O'Grady said, "and certainly not why."

"Damn it all," Wheeler said, "this is goddamned inconvenient."

O'Grady thought that there might be a stronger word to describe having been shot in the back, but decided to let inconvenient cover it, for now.

"What did you tell the police?"

He told Wheeler exactly what he had told Inspector Names.

"Well, I didn't let on that we knew each other," Wheeler said, "and I certainly haven't told him anything damaging."

"How are we going to handle this, sir?" O'Grady asked.

"Handle what?"

"The shooting, sir," O'Grady said. "How do we find out who did it."

"Damn it all, man!" Wheeler said, then lowered his voice. "We've got more important things to worry about. Did you keep your appointment with Arthur Doyle?"

"Yes, sir."

"And."

"Well, sir, I didn't know when I'd be able to talk to you—"

"Yes, yes?"

"—and Mr. Doyle did seem to need a swift reply, so—"

"Yes?"

"—I told him I'd do it."

"Do what, damn it?"

"Sir?"

"What specifically did you tell him you would do?" Wheeler asked, impatiently.

"Well, I told him I'd go to Mexico and pay the ransom, and get his daughter."

"Well, you're certainly not!"

"Sir?"

"Damn it, I *told* you not to give him a decision—"

"Sir, you weren't in any condition—at least, I didn't think you were—"

"All right, all right," Wheeler said, "it's my damned fault for getting shot."

"I didn't say—"

"Never mind," Wheeler said. "I will tell you exactly what you *are* going to do."

"All right, sir."

"You're going to go to Mexico and get that girl away from those revolutionaries—"

"Sir, that's what I said—"

"—but you will *not* pay them a red cent!"

"Excuse me?"

41

"Damn it, man, do you know what Fuljencio will be able to do with a million American dollars."

"Well, for one thing he could forget all about the revolution and retire."

"Not likely," Wheeler said. "Fuljencio is a zealot. He actually believes that the people of Mexico will be better off with him as President."

"Ah," O'Grady said, getting the idea, "but the United States Government doesn't agree."

"No, it doesn't," Wheeler said, "so the one thing you will *not* do is pay the ransom."

"Sir," O'Grady asked, "which part of this comes under the heading of a favor, and which comes under the heading of an order."

Wheeler shifted, trying to get comfortable.

"Officially, the United States government cannot get involved," Wheeler said. "I can only ask you to go into Mexico and do what I . . . I asked you to do."

"I see."

"If you're caught, we will have to disavow any knowledge of you."

"Uh-huh," O'Grady said. "And what about manpower?"

"You'll have to supply your own," Wheeler said. "We're taking chance enough sending you in. You'll have to get your own people."

"Preferably people who are not connected with the United States government in any way."

"Correct."

"Mmm," O'Grady said. He walked to the window and looked outside. "Well, it's certainly a challenge."

"I would say," Wheeler said. "Fuljencio has a couple of hundred men under his command."

"Two hundred, huh?"

"Oh, from what we know, about forty of them are

trained soldiers, and the others are volunteers—farmers, mostly."

"Still," O'Grady said, "forty trained men . . ."

"Yes," Wheeler said. "Well, what do you say?"

"I've already given my decision to Mr. Doyle, sir," O'Grady said, "and I can't go back on that now."

"Good," Wheeler said, "then you'll do it."

"Well . . . I'll have to take his money with me. I mean, you don't want him to know that we're *not* going to pay the ransom."

"God, no," Wheeler said. "I hope he never finds that out."

"Well, he won't find out from me, sir."

"Will you be able to get some people together in time?" Wheeler asked.

"Well . . . just by coincidence, we're in exactly the city that makes it easy for me to do that."

"We can supply you with some funds," Wheeler said, "but not enough to put an army together."

"I won't need an army, sir."

"Well, you'll need at least twenty trained men—" Wheeler started.

"I was thinking more along the lines of five," O'Grady said, interrupting him.

"What? Five men?"

"Ah . . . five people," O'Grady said, because one of the people he was thinking of was a woman.

"Are you mad?" Wheeler said. "What can you do with five people?"

"Well, sir," O'Grady said, smiling, "I guess that would depend on who they are, wouldn't it?"

"Jesus Christ, man, you're smiling like the cat that swallowed the canary. What have you got on your mind?"

"Just something I've been wondering about for a

long time, sir," O'Grady said, "and I think I'm finally going to have the chance to satisfy my curiosity."

"If you're not going to talk sense you'd better get out of here and let me sleep."

"Yes, sir," O'Grady said, "I know you need your rest. I'm glad to see that you're feeling . . . all right."

"Yes, well, the doctors claim they saved my life," Wheeler said, sleepily, "but I had no intention of dying in the first place."

Or the second place, Canyon O'Grady would wager.

6

O'Grady returned to his hotel, wondering if he could ever attach so little importance to being shot as Rufus Wheeler seemed to have done.

As he entered the hotel he saw Inspector Names waiting in the lobby, presumably for him.

"Inspector," he said. "What can I do for you?"

"I was wondering, Mr. O'Grady," Names said, "if anything else had come back to you since the last time we spoke."

O'Grady had the feeling the inspector was trying to catch him in something.

"Well, I just came from the hospital, so I now know that the man I had lunch with is named Wheeler."

"Just Wheeler?"

"You know something," O'Grady said, "I didn't ask what his first name was? When it comes to names I'm just—"

"Yes, yes," Names said, "I know. Why, you probably don't even remember who you had dinner with tonight, do you?"

"Why, Inspector," O'Grady said, his tone meant to take the inspector to task, "I do believe you're having me watched."

"Never mind that," Names said. "I'm interested in your dinner companion."

"You already know that it was Arthur Doyle."

"What were you doing with one of Denver's richest citizens?" the policeman asked.

O'Grady frowned and asked, "What does that have to do with the shooting of Mr. Wheeler?"

"It has to do with you, Mr. O'Grady."

"Excuse me, Inspector," O'Grady said, "but I don't think what I had for dinner, or who I had dinner with, is any of your business."

"Now listen here—"

"I suggest that if you want to know about my dinner with Mr. Doyle, you ask him," O'Grady said. "If you want to talk to me any further, I'm afraid you will have to take me to your headquarters. If not, I am going to bed. I've had a trying day."

Names stared at O'Grady for a few moments, then said, "Remember not to leave Denver without checking with me first, Mr. O'Grady."

"Don't worry, Inspector," O'Grady said, "you'll be the first to know my travel plans."

"Just make sure of it," Names said, and walked away. O'Grady waited until the man had left the hotel, then walked to the desk.

"Are there any messages for me?" he asked.

He didn't expect that there would be, but while the clerk checked he took the opportunity to turn and lean against the desk and check the lobby out. It was a big lobby, and there were always people coming and going, to their rooms, to and from the restaurant or the hotel bar. It was *too* big a lobby for him to pick out his tail. He had to get who ever it was into a smaller space.

"I'm sorry, sir," the clerk said, "no messages. Were you expecting—"

"No," O'Grady said, "as a matter of fact I *wasn't* expecting any, I just wanted to check. Thank you."

Instead of going up to his room, he crossed the

lobby, bypassing the restaurant, and entered the hotel bar.

The bar was smaller than the lobby, but there were more people here. This wasn't going to help much, either, unless he stayed late, waiting for the place to empty out.

He decided against that, but also decided that while he was there he might as well have a beer. He walked to the bar, ordered the beer and watched the entrance through the mirror behind the bar. Nobody came in behind him. He frowned. Could Names have had a man in the lobby, and one in the bar? *And* one in the restaurant? If so, why was the inspector assigning so much manpower to watch him? Because he had lunch with Wheeler before he was shot? Because he had dinner with Arthur Doyle? No, that wasn't it. He was *seen* with Doyle, which meant he was already being watched by that time.

Names must have figured that there was more to the O'Grady/Wheeler lunch than he was being told. Of course, the man was right. He was probably very good at his job, and if he thought something was being kept from him, he wasn't going to walk away from it. He was going to dig and dig until he unearthed something.

O'Grady wondered what they could give him that would satisfy him? He'd have to approach Wheeler with the question in the morning.

O'Grady finished his beer, declined another and left the bar. He walked across the lobby, still alert for anyone paying him special attention, but by the time he reached the stairway he still hadn't spotted anyone. If Inspector Names was a good policeman, the men he was using to watch O'Grady must have been good, as well.

Tomorrow, on the street, was when O'Grady would

probably be able to identify someone. Tonight he was going to stop trying, and get some sleep. He had asked Doyle to give him three days because his intention *had* been to snoop around to try and find out who shot Wheeler. Now he figured he'd go and see Doyle tomorrow to discuss the situation a little further—including what Doyle should tell Names—and then he'd try to collect his people before the three days was up.

In his room O'Grady undressed then slipped between the cool, crisp, fresh sheets and noticed that Linda Church's scent was still hanging in the air. It was the first time he had thought about her since that morning.

Lying on his back, staring up at the ceiling, he mentally put his five-"person" team together for the rescue attempt of Anja Doyle.

The man he wanted first was an old friend of his, Francis "Preacher" O'Mara. Frank O'Mara was a real preacher who was also the fastest man O'Grady had ever seen with a gun. Along with Skye Fargo, O'Mara was the man O'Grady would rather have backing him in a gunfight. O'Mara was about thirty-five years old, and was also more than a little bit crazy.

Adam Shea was next. Shea was in his thirties, and was a genius with explosives.

Jack "Blackjack" Decker was a gambler, and a con man. It was his abilities as a con man that O'Grady thought he could put to use. The man was in his forties, but could pass for younger or older any time he wanted to, and could look like two different people from one minute to the next.

C.K. Fletcher was only in his early twenties, and he looked younger. In fact, Fletcher's baby face was his greatest asset, because no one would suspect him of being capable of anything, when in reality, he *was* capable of anything.

The last person he wanted was the lovely Jinx Quinones. Jinx was handy with a gun, and was not above using her considerable charms to get what she wanted. She was half Spanish—that was *Spanish*, not Mexican—and half American, and she and O'Grady had an odd sort of relationship that could almost be described as love-hate.

With these five people—most of whom straddled the line between right and wrong—O'Grady felt he could get almost anything done. O'Mara and Shea knew each other, but other than that the five were strangers to each other, and O'Grady had often wondered what would happen if he brought them all together in the same place. Now he was going to be able to find out.

The advantageous aspect of his plan was that O'Mara worked out of Denver, and would be able to find Shea wherever he was. O'Grady knew where he could leave messages for Decker, Fletcher and Jinx Quinones, but he wasn't going to wait for a reply. He'd give them their meeting point—somewhere in Texas, just this side of the border—and when he got there he'd find out if they were in or out.

Satisfied that his private army was assembled—at least in his mind—he turned over and went right to sleep.

The next morning, O'Grady went to church.

It was a weathered wooden structure that had once been abandoned. When Preacher O'Mara took it over he didn't spend very much money fixing it up. He didn't *have* very much money, but he managed to lure a flock into his church, which he called the Church of the Holy Avenger.

O'Grady stood in the back of the church and waited for Preacher to finish firing up his flock, and when the collection basket came around he dropped some money into it, and a note.

O'Grady waited outside while the flock filed out, and the last person out was O'Mara.

"Canyon, my friend," O'Mara said.

O'Grady turned and accepted the proffered hand. O'Mara wore a dark suit, and on his hip was his ever-present .45 with worn wooden grips.

"Preacher."

"To what do I owe this pleasure?"

"Is there somewhere we can talk?"

"Sure," Preacher said, "business or pleasure?"

"Preacher . . ." O'Grady said.

"Business," Preacher said. "Come with me."

Preacher led O'Grady through the church into a small back room, where there was an old wooden desk with three legs, and a pair of mismatched wooden chairs.

"I have nothing to offer you in the way of refreshment," Preacher said, apologetically.

"That's all right."

"What's on your mind?"

O'Grady took a couple of seconds to study his old friend. Preacher O'Mara had prematurely white hair, which he wore long, and together with his pale skin it almost gave him an albinolike appearance. Anyone who saw him coming their way would cross the street to avoid passing too close to him. Yet, when he was in the pulpit, people's attention was riveted to him.

"I've got a job," O'Grady said.

"Does it pay?" O'Mara asked. "I'm not asking for myself, you understand, but my flock . . ."

"I understand," O'Grady said. "I'm sure proper payment could be arranged." It might even come out of the million Doyle supplied for the ransom.

"Then pray tell me . . ." O'Mara said.

O'Grady outlined the assignment—"favor" for him, "job" for Preacher, but O'Grady still thought of it as an assignment—and Preacher O'Mara listened intently.

"Who else will you be, uh, drafting for this suicide mission?"

"Shea," O'Grady said, "if you can find him."

"I'll find him."

"Blackjack Decker, Jinx Quinones and C.K. Fletcher."

"Decker and the Quinones woman I have heard of," Preacher said, "but who is Fletcher?"

"He's a youngster with some talent," O'Grady said, "don't worry about him. What do you say, Preacher, in or out?"

Preacher raised one hand and showed O'Grady his long forefinger. He was about to make a point.

"Not for myself," he said, slowly, "but for my flock, and for the poor, unfortunate young woman who has been taken by the heathen—"

"Preacher!"

"I'm in, Canyon," Preacher said with a serene smile, "I am in."

7

O'Grady left it to Preacher to get ahold of Adam
Shea, and they agreed to meet at the Denver House
Hotel that evening. Leaving the Church of the Holy
Avenger, Canyon knew that when the word got back
to Inspector Names about *that* meeting the policeman
would find it *very* interesting. During his trip to the
Church, O'Grady still was not able to identify his tail,
a fact which was starting to bother him. He was usually able to tell when he was being followed, and
would have liked to meet the man who was following
him so successfully.

When O'Grady left the church he hailed a horse-
drawn cab and gave the driver Arthur Doyle's address. If the driver recognized the address he gave no
indication. He had decided to see Doyle first and warn
him about Inspector Names's involvement before he
went to the hospital to see how Wheeler was.

Doyle's house was an impressive two-story brick
structure, but O'Grady paid more attention to the fact
that there was a uniformed policeman on the porch.
As he mounted the porch the policeman looked at
him, but did not speak to him. O'Grady knocked on
the door and waited. It was answered by black man
who was either the butler, or the houseboy, or house-
man, O'Grady didn't know which.

"Yes, sir?"

"My name is Canyon O'Grady—"

"Oh, yes sir," the man said, "come right in." The man spoke perfect English. "I will tell Mr. Doyle you are here."

"Is there a Inspector Names with him?" O'Grady asked.

"Why, yes, sir."

O'Grady considered the wisdom of asking the man to let him wait somewhere out of sight, and then decided against it. The policeman on the porch had already seen him.

"All right," he said, finally, "you can tell him I'm here."

"Yes, sir," the black man said, and went off down a hallway, his footsteps echoing.

O'Grady remained in the entry foyer of the house, looking at the sweeping set of stairs that led to the second floor.

In a few minutes he heard three sets of footsteps returning. In moments the black man appeared with Arthur Doyle, and Inspector Names.

"Good morning, Mr. O'Grady," Doyle said.

O'Grady couldn't help but wonder what Doyle had said to Names about their meeting yesterday.

"Mr. Doyle," O'Grady said. " 'Morning, Inspector."

"What a coincidence meeting you here," Names said.

"Not much of a coincidence when you think about it," O'Grady said.

"I suppose not."

"Inspector?" Doyle said. "Have we finished our business?" Doyle's tone made it clear that he thought they had. It was odd to see the dumpy Doyle forcing the inspector to back down.

"Yes, sir, I believe that we have," Names said. The

look the policeman gave O'Grady plainly said that *they* had not finished *their* business.

The black man opened the door for Names, who almost reluctantly walked out.

"Come with me," Doyle said, and led the way back down the same hallway until they reached his office, which was surprisingly small, but expensively furnished.

"I came to warn you about him," O'Grady said.

"I know how to handle minor officials like the inspector," Doyle said.

"What did he want to know?"

"Our business," Doyle said, "which I told him was not *his* business."

"How did he take that?"

Doyle looked impatient to be spending time talking about Names.

"I phrased it somewhat diplomatically," Doyle said. O'Grady was sure that Doyle was good at *that*.

"What have you come here to tell me?" Doyle asked.

"Well, first I came to ask you to have your doctor look at Wheeler. You offered last night, but we never got around to it."

"Yes, of course," Doyle said, looking for something to write on. "What hospital is he at."

"He's at the Holy Name Hospital," O'Grady said, "which I understand you are a patron of."

"Yes," Doyle said, "it's an excellent hospital." He didn't have to write down the name. "I'll have my doctor get right over there."

"Thank you."

"Now . . . what have you come to talk about? Do you still need those three days?"

"I'll need the days to put together the people I'll be taking to Texas with me."

"People? For what?"

"I'll need someone to back me up."

"O'Grady," Doyle said, "you won't do anything to endanger my daughter's life, will you?"

"Mr. Doyle, that's the last thing I'd want to do."

"I believe you," Doyle said, "but what about your bosses?"

"Rufus Wheeler is my boss, Mr. Doyle, and right now he's out of commission. This is going to be my show, and I'll be bringing my own people in. There's just one thing I need from you."

"What's that?"

"Money."

"Really?" Doyle said, looking skeptical.

"Not for me," O'Grady said, "but for the people I bring in. They'll be doing this for pay."

"I'll cover whatever your expenses are, of course," Doyle said.

"Okay," O'Grady said.

"When will you need the ransom money?"

"Probably tomorrow night or the following morning. I'll pick it up here. Make the bills as large as possible, so that the package is as small as possible."

"Very well. Will you be able to get your people here in time?"

"Some of them are here already," O'Grady said, "and some of them will meet us in Texas."

"I want to make something very clear here, Mr. O'Grady," Doyle said, with some steel in his voice *and* in his back.

"What's that, sir?"

"My daughter's freedom, and her life, take precedence over anything. I don't care what the United States government wants out of this—don't interrupt me, please. I'm quite aware that Rufus Wheeler will have his own agenda here. If my daughter is not freed, indeed, if she is killed, the government will be extremely unhappy—I will see to it."

"I'll pass that along."

"I won't be very happy with you, either, Mr. O'Grady," Doyle added.

"Mr. Doyle," O'Grady said, gruffly, "you can make Inspector Names back down, and probably as many minor officials as you want, but remember one thing. There's nothing in this for me, absolutely nothing. I want to get your daughter out of there, and no amount of threats from you is going to make me want that *more* than I do now."

Doyle stood there for a few moments, and then abruptly slumped.

"I apologize," Doyle said, "I'm . . . distraught—"

"There's no need to go any further," O'Grady said. "I'll send you a message when to have the money ready to go."

"Yes, all right."

"We'll probably see each other one more time, Mr. Doyle," O'Grady said. "I'll need that expense money, as well."

"How much?"

O'Grady thought a moment, then said, "Give me fifty thousand as an advance against final payment to my people."

"All right."

"If my people are killed," O'Grady said, "I'll still want their payment. It will go to next of kin."

"Of course, of course," Doyle said. "Just get my daughter back . . . please."

"We'll do our best, Mr. Doyle," O'Grady said. "That's all we can do."

8

When O'Grady got to the hospital, Sister Madrid was *not* behind the desk, but the young nun he had met yesterday, Sister Marie, was.

"Hi," he said, "remember me?"

She looked up at him, smiled and said, "How could I forget?"

He wondered what, if anything, that meant.

"Can I see my friend?"

"There's another doctor examining him right now," she said. "Can you wait?"

"Sure."

O'Grady figured that had to be Arthur Doyle's doctor. But he had come here straight from Doyle's house. How could Doyle have gotten his doctor here so quickly, unless he had *already* made the arrangements.

O'Grady sat on the bench in the lobby until Sister Marie told him he could go back to the room.

"Do you remember the way?"

"Yes," he said, wondering if he had said "no" if she would have shown him the way herself.

When he got to the room Wheeler was lying in much the same position he had been in the night before. As he entered the room Wheeler's glare was like something physical, and O'Grady wondered what he had done to deserve it.

"Were you responsible for this?" Wheeler demanded.

"For what . . . sir?"

"That new doctor that came in here and examined me," Wheeler said. "That was Arthur Doyle's doctor."

"It was?" The way Wheeler said "Arthur Doyle" O'Grady was sure there was something beneath the surface here which might be bubbling to the top.

"Don't play games with me, O'Grady," Wheeler said. "Did you have Doyle send his doctor here today?"

It only took O'Grady a moment to decide that he really *didn't* have anything to do with it, because Doyle had obviously made the arrangements *before* their meeting that morning.

So when he said, "No, sir," he was technically telling the truth.

"Well . . ." Wheeler said, not sure that he believed the big redhaired agent.

"What's the problem with Doyle's doctor coming to see you?"

Wheeler looked at O'Grady and then muttered, "It's something . . . personal. I don't want to get into now."

There was *something* between Doyle and Wheeler that O'Grady didn't know about, but he had no time to try to pry it out of his boss.

"Have you gotten your people together?" Wheeler asked.

"Two of them," O'Grady said. "I'll be sending three telegrams off this afternoon."

"Are they reliable?"

"They're all good at what they do," O'Grady said, hedging.

"They're all like you, then," Wheeler said, "is that what you're trying to say?"

"What about the person who shot you?" O'Grady asked, deciding not to comment.

"What about him?"

"What's being done to find him?"

"I suppose the inspector is doing all he can," Wheeler said. "I'll get a telegram off as soon as I can to Washington, and we'll get some people on it. Don't concern yourself with it, O'Grady. Do you understand? You've got enough to do."

"Yes, sir," O'Grady said. "I understand."

"Well then, get out of here and do it," Wheeler said. "Stop spending so much time at this hospital."

"Yes, sir."

O'Grady left the hospital wondering which man would finally tell him what the bone of contention was, Wheeler or Doyle?

The Denver House had their own facilities for sending telegraph messages, so O'Grady went back there and sent his messages to Blackjack Decker, C.K. Fletcher and Jinx Quinones. He hoped that Jinx would respond favorably and meet him and Preacher and Shea in the Texas town he had chosen as their meeting place.

After all his attempts to discover who was watching him, it happened by accident that he identified two of the men. Apparently, as he was walking through the lobby, two of the policeman watching him had decided to converse and, when O'Grady appeared, they were in a quandary as to how to play it. They finally decided to move away from each other and pretend not to know each other, but the move was so abrupt that O'Grady couldn't help but catch it. *Both* men were familiar to him, as he had probably seen them before in the bar or the restaurant, or even in the lobby or on the street. He continued walking, pretending that he had not seen them, but he had now successfully identified two of the men who were assigned to watch him.

Their attempt to keep him from noticing them was so badly played, however, that he doubted that either of them was the man who was following him *outside* the hotel. Rather, these two men had been assigned to watch him while he was *inside* the hotel. The man who was following him outside was the man O'Grady was impressed with, and the one he would like to have met.

After leaving the messages, O'Grady went back to his room to consider his next move. He had Preacher and, presumably, Adam Shea meeting him at the hotel later in the evening. He *could* have had them meet him elsewhere, but he figured why bother. They weren't doing anything illegal, and Inspector Names could question them all he wanted.

Preacher usually kept his life in Denver as leader of his flock separate from his life *away* from Denver, where he was virtually a mercenary for hire. That meant that Names might not know who the Preacher was. Shea, who also often frequented Denver, though he didn't live here, did not ply his trade in the city, either. Names, however, might become interested in them simply because they were meeting with O'Grady. Perhaps he *should* have had them meet him elsewhere, but it was too later now to change it. Hopefully, Names would not continue to be interested in them once O'Grady left Denver.

Looking out his window, O'Grady realized that he was looking at the building across the street from the Denver House hotel. He doubted that the shot that felled Wheeler could have come from street level.

That meant that the shooter had to either be in a room in that building, or on the roof.

He decided to have a look.

As it turned out, the building was also a hotel, though not on the grand scale of the Denver House. He was able to make his way to the roof, where he walked to the front and looked down on the street. The shooter would have had to set up somewhere along here if he hadn't used a room—and O'Grady doubted that he had. There would have been more chance of being seen if he used a room.

O'Grady was sure the police had already been up here, but he looked around, anyway. There was some scuffing on the ledge in several places, but there was no evidence that anyone had been up there recently. It had either been removed or, whoever the shooter was, he as too good to have left any.

O'Grady decided to go back across the street and nurse a beer or two until Preacher and Shea arrived.

Before leaving the hotel he stopped at the desk. He remembered Wheeler saying that he was *not* registered in the Denver House, but in another hotel. O'Grady didn't know if Wheeler would have registered under his real name, but there was no harm in asking. As it turned out, he had.

"Can you tell me what room he's in?"

"Well, sir—"

"He's in the hospital, you know," O'Grady said.

"Really?" the clerk said.

"That shooting that took place across the street yesterday."

"Was that him?"

"Yes."

"The poor man," the young clerk said. "He's not dead, is he?"

"No," O'Grady said, "but he asked me to stop and pick up some things in his room."

"I see," the clerk said. "Well, I guess there's no harm in telling you, then. He's in room five-oh-three."

"Does that room look out on the front of the hotel?"

"Why yes, it does."

"Can I have a key, please?"

"He didn't give you a key?" the clerk asked, skeptically.

"Would you believe it?" O'Grady said. "The hospital lost his hotel key."

"I see."

To help the young man along in his decision O'Grady took some money out of his pocket and laid a bill on the desk. It was gone instantly, before anyone else could see it.

"Here you go, sir," the clerk said, setting the key down on the desk. "Five-oh-three."

"Yes," O'Grady said, "thank you."

He took the key up to the fifth floor and let himself into the room. The room was a mess, which confirmed what he suspected. The shooter had set up here, *knowing* that the room would be empty. O'Grady moved to the window and looked down, and he had a perfect view of the front of the Denver House, where Wheeler was shot.

There was no evidence left behind here, but O'Grady knew that Wheeler would never have left his room in such a mess. It had obviously been searched, and that brought up a wealth of questions, which O'Grady lifted in his mind one at a time.

What were they searching for?

And why?

Did the search and the shooting have anything to do with Anja Doyle's kidnapping?

Had *Generalisimo* Fuljencio sent someone to Denver to watch Doyle? And if so, how did they get onto Wheeler?

Or had it been Wheeler who been followed from Washington? If he was, then someone knew that there was a connection between Wheeler and Doyle, and they *knew* Doyle would go to the government—or Wheeler—for help.

Somebody knew a lot more about what was going on than O'Grady did . . . and that was going to change.

9

O'Grady went back across the street, still moving the questions around in his mind like the pieces of a puzzle, hoping that they would eventually fall into place. Over his first beer he realized that they would *never* fall into place if neither Wheeler or Doyle ever talked to him.

If someone knew that Wheeler was here to help Doyle, did they then know about O'Grady? Surely, they would have seen him have lunch with Wheeler, and dinner with Arthur Doyle. If someone *did* know about him, then that meant he could be next on the shooter's list.

Over the second beer he decided that it might be time for him to change hotels.

He wondered how Inspector Names was going to feel about that?

O'Grady decided to try to intercept Preacher and Shea outside the hotel. What he had to do was somehow get outside without the two inside men seeing him and alerting the outside man. Of course, having identified the two inside men gave him the edge.

He decided to use the fact that he had been seen in the dining room last night with Arthur Doyle.

"Excuse me," he said to the maitre d', the same man he had seen on duty the night before.

The man looked at him and immediately recognized him as having been with Doyle.

"Yes, sir?"

"I was here last night with Mr. Doyle?" O'Grady said, unnecessarily.

"Of course, sir, I remember."

"Mr. Doyle would like me to look at your kitchen."

The man hesitated, then blinked and said, "I beg your pardon?"

"I have to see your kitchen."

"Uh, was there something wrong with the food last night, sir? If Mr. Doyle had any complaints—"

"The only complaint he's going to have," O'Grady said, "is if you don't let me see your kitchen."

"Well . . ." the man said, "well . . . of course, if Mr. Doyle wants you to see the kitchen, I will show you the kitchen."

"Thank you," O'Grady said.

"Follow me, please."

O'Grady followed the man across the dining room floor and into the kitchen, which appeared to be spotless. O'Grady wasn't looking for dirt, though. He was looking for a door that led to the outside.

"Where does that door go?" he asked the man.

"That door leads outside, sir."

"I see."

"Is everything all right, sir?"

"Oh, everything is fine, just fine," O'Grady said, and the man looked relieved. "What's your name?"

"Marcel, sir."

"All right, Marcel, you can go back to the dining room. If you don't mind, I'm going to go out this way."

"Uh, no, sir, I don't, er, mind at all."

"Thank you, Marcel," O'Grady said. "I'll tell Mr. Doyle that you cooperated fully."

"Thank you, sir."

O'Grady waited for the man to leave and then moved to the kitchen door and left that way, while the kitchen crew stared after him curiously.

Outside, he had to guess as to which direction Preacher and Shea would come from. He simply picked the direction of Preacher's church, assuming that the men would come from there. He had only to wait a short while before he saw Preacher, who was very easy to spot from far off due to his black clothing and white hair.

The man at his side was shorter by a considerable margin. Adam Shea stood only about five nine, but when it came to women his lack of height was no detriment. He was not particularly handsome, but he knew how to talk to women, and how to treat them, and they responded to him.

O'Grady did not wait for them to reach him, but moved to intercept them a half a block from the hotel.

"O'Grady—" Shea said with a smile when he saw the big redhead.

"Not here," O'Grady said, cutting him off. "I'm being watched by the police. Do you have someplace we can talk, Preacher?"

"Do they know about me?" Preacher asked.

"No."

"We could go to my church."

"I'd rather go someplace where we can get a drink and talk," Shea said.

"Demon rum—" Preacher started, but O'Grady cut him off.

"Preach later, Preacher," he said. "Take us someplace."

"Very well," Preacher said. "Come with me." He reversed his direction and they went back the way he and Shea had come.

*   *   *

Preacher took them to a small saloon far from the hotel. There was no chance that they would accidentally be found by the police.

"Preacher tells me you have a job for us," Shea said when they were seated with drinks in front of them. Both Shea and O'Grady had beer, while Preacher had a glass of milk.

"That's right."

"Does this job pay well?"

"It will."

"Up front?"

"Some up front, and then rest when the job is done," O'Grady said.

"And if we don't live until the end of the job?" Shea asked.

"The money will go to whoever you say."

"My flock," Preacher said.

"I want it buried with me," Shea said, giving Preacher a look. "Why don't you have yours given to your surviving friends?"

"What friends?" Preacher asked, and Shea gave him a look.

"All right, never mind," O'Grady said. "Did you tell him about it?" he asked Preacher.

"I thought I would leave that to you."

"Yeah," Shea said, "tell me about it."

O'Grady outlined the job and Shea grew more and more distressed as he listened.

"Wait a minute," he said, when O'Grady was finished, "let me get this straight. We have to defeat an entire Mexican army, and bring the girl out alive?"

"We don't have to defeat them," O'Grady said, "we just have to bring the girl out . . . alive."

"And how much do we get paid for this?" Shea asked.

"A lot."

"And how many of us will there be?"

"Six," O'Grady said.

"Is that *in*cluding you, or *ex*cluding you?" Shea asked after a moment.

"Including me."

"This is crazy."

"No, it is not," O'Grady said. "It will be worth it to you."

"If I survive," Shea said.

"Of course."

Shea looked at Preacher and said, "Are you in?"

"I'm in."

Shea gave both of them looks that said they were crazy, then shrugged, smiled and said, "Okay, I'm in, too."

"Good."

"Who else is involved?"

"Blackjack Decker, C.K. Fletcher and Jinx Quinones," O'Grady said.

"I've heard of Decker," Shea said. "Who are the other two?"

O'Grady told him.

"A woman?" Shea said. "You're bringing a woman into this?"

"She'll carry her weight," O'Grady said.

"Jesus," Shea said, "A woman." He shook his head, then asked. "Is she good-looking."

"Extremely."

"You have sin on your mind, brother," Preacher said to Shea.

"*And* in my heart, Preacher," Shea said, nodding.

"*And* in your soul," Preacher said.

"I don't have a soul," Shea said.

"Blasphemer."

"Can we get on with this?" O'Grady asked.

Both Preacher and Shea gave him their attention.

"I want both of you to leave on a train tomorrow. I'll come a day later. We'll be meeting the others in a town called Medallion. It's near the Pecos River. You know the place, Preacher."

Preacher just nodded.

"The others are meeting us there?" Shea asked.

"Yes."

"How will we know them."

"You won't," O'Grady said. "Just wait for me to get there. Don't try to make contact with anyone, because it may be the wrong person."

"Do they know about us?" Shea asked.

"No."

"We'll need money for train tickets," Preacher said, "and then horses."

"We'll meet tomorrow afternoon and I'll have some expense money for you. Meanwhile, I'll give you the money for the tickets."

He took out his wallet and gave the money to Preacher. He'd reimburse himself from the fifty thousand he'd be getting from Doyle tomorrow.

"What are we gonna need in the way of supplies?" Shea asked.

"I'll make a list," O'Grady said. They got paper and pencil from the bartender and he wrote down everything they would need, including the explosives he wanted Shea to collect.

Shea took the list, read it, grinned and said, "Ooh, toys."

"Just make sure you don't blow us up with the stuff," O'Grady said.

Shea looked hurt and said, "Hey, O'Grady, you forget, you're talking to a master."

"Don't worry," Preacher said, "the Lord will keep us safe."

"Sure," Shea said.

"And if he starts to play games," Preacher added, "I'll break his arms."

10

When O'Grady returned to the hotel, Inspector Names was waiting in the lobby. This was not totally unexpected. When his men reported that O'Grady had disappeared from the hotel, the inspector was sure to come to the hotel to wait for him. As he entered, Names approached him forcefully.

"What the hell is going on?"

"I don't know what you mean, Inspector."

"You damn well do know what I mean," the policeman said. "You avoided my men and left the hotel."

"I remember you telling me not to leave town, Inspector," O'Grady said, "but I don't remember being told that I could not leave the hotel. If your men were unable to stay with me, that's not my problem."

Names opened his mouth to argue the point, then abruptly closed it. To say more would be to admit that he was having O'Grady watched and he didn't want to do that, just as O'Grady didn't want to admit that he had spotted the two men inside the hotel. That would have told Names that O'Grady was much more than he presented himself to be.

"Was there something you wanted to talk to me about tonight, Inspector?" O'Grady asked, innocently.

"You've been to see Mr. Wheeler in the hospital?" Names finally asked.

"Yes."

"Why do I get the feeling that you and he know more about this shooting incident than you're telling?" the inspector asked.

"I don't know, Inspector," O'Grady said, "why is that?"

"O'Grady . . ." Names said, at a loss for the words to say what he really wanted to say, " . . . if I find out whatever it is you don't want me to find out—"

"Talk to Wheeler, Inspector," O'Grady said. "He's the one who got shot, he's the one who should know *why* he got shot. I just had lunch with the man."

"And dinner with the wealthiest man in Denver," Names reminded him.

O'Grady frowned and said, "Is that what's really bothering you, Inspector? That I had dinner—that I was a *guest* at dinner with Arthur Doyle? Why is that?"

"Because you're here to do something you don't want me to know about," Names said. "When people try to hide things from me it makes my nose twitch, it make my hands ache . . . it makes me want to know that much more what's going on."

"If you want to know what's going on, ask Doyle," O'Grady said.

"Ask Doyle," Names said, "ask Wheeler, *they* know what's going on. You're just an innocent bystander, isn't that right?"

O'Grady spread his hands helplessly and said, "That's exactly right, Inspector."

"No," Names said, "no, it isn't. You're no gambler, O'Grady—at least, not the kind you're trying to represent yourself to be. For one thing, I haven't seen you involved in any kind of game."

"I'm on holiday, Inspector," O'Grady said. "Even gamblers have to take vacations."

"The more you try to convince me, the more convinced I become otherwise," Names said. "I'll still be watching you, O'Grady."

As Names strode out of the hotel, O'Grady thought, not for long. He wondered how Names was going to react when he found out that O'Grady had left Denver—which was what he planned to do day after tomorrow.

All he had to do now was come up with a plan to get away from the hotel, and Names' men, and get on a train without anyone seeing him.

As he walked the rest of the way through the lobby he looked for Names' men and didn't see them. No doubt, Names had already replaced them, and now O'Grady would have to identify them all over again.

O'Grady went to his room and stayed there until the next morning, when he left the hotel to go to Arthur Doyle's home.

As he knocked on Doyle's door he wondered if the man had an office, or if he simply worked out of his home. The same black man answered the door, bid him good morning and showed him the way to Doyle's den.

"Good morning, Mr. O'Grady," Doyle said from behind his desk. He pushed a thick white envelope across the desk. "There is your expense money. The million will be at your disposal at a moment's notice."

"Let's make it a bank draft, Mr. Doyle," O'Grady said. "Why take the chance of traveling with that much cash."

Doyle frowned and said, "I prefer dealing with cash."

"Won't your draft be honored by a Texas bank?" O'Grady asked.

"Of course," Doyle said. "Any bank in Lubbock,

or Abilene, Dallas or Odessa. That will not be a problem for you."

"Fine," O'Grady said. He had thought about this on the way over. He picked up the envelope filled with fifty thousand dollars and said, "Prepare the draft. I'll pick it up tonight."

"Very well."

"Now, I need you to have someone buy me a train ticket. The police are still watching me. I'm sure they followed me here."

Doyle looked annoyed.

"I can have that stopped, you know."

O'Grady raised his hand and said, "Let it go. I don't need any extra pressure from Inspector Names."

"I mean, I can have the pressure taken *off*."

"Excuse me for saying so, Mr. Doyle," O'Grady said, "but the more you try to have the pressure taken off, the more pressure Inspector Names will put on. He's a good policeman. Instead of flexing your muscles at him, you should try and get him over to your side."

Doyle seemed to consider the suggestion and then said, "I'll keep that in mind."

"I'll pick up the bank draft and the ticket tonight," O'Grady said.

He gave Doyle the information as to what route he wanted to take to get to Texas, and then made arrangements for his horse, Cormac, to be picked up and taken to the station.

"If I can help you in any way," Doyle said, "perhaps a diversion to get you away from the hotel, let me know."

O'Grady said, "Let me think about that. I might come up with a plan by tonight. If not, then I will need your help."

"I will be ready," Doyle said. "I have men at my disposal."

O'Grady started to leave, then stopped and said, "Can I ask you something?"

"Of course."

"You just said something interesting to me," O'Grady said. "You just said that you have men at your disposal."

"Yes."

"I mean, rich men, they always have the money to buy men to do what they want, right?"

Doyle frowned and said, "I suppose."

"Why not this time?" O'Grady asked. "Why didn't you just buy some men of your own and send them in to get your daughter?"

"That's a fairly simple question to answer," Doyle said. "When it comes to my business, I know what men to buy and what they can do. I did not trust myself in this instance to buy the right men for the job."

"So you left it to Rufus Wheeler," O'Grady said.

"That's right."

"How did you know that Wheeler would help you?"

Doyle allowed himself a small smile and said, "I really did not give him much choice."

"No," O'Grady said, "that's not right. You didn't give the United States *government* much of a choice. Rufus Wheeler had a choice, but he chose to come . . . even though I get the impression that you don't like each other."

Doyle stared at O'Grady for a few moments and then said, "Mr. O'Grady, have a seat."

O'Grady sat.

11

"If I understand you correctly, you're wondering about my relationship with Rufus Wheeler."

"I'm wondering what it is about you that he dislikes so much."

"Well, that could easily be my money—but you know Rufus, so you wouldn't believe that, would you?"

"No, sir."

"Very well, then," Doyle said, "if it's not money that is a bone of contention between men, than what else could it be?"

It took O'Grady only a moment to come up with the answer.

"A woman?"

Doyle nodded.

"A woman . . . Anja's mother. You see, when Rufus and I were at the Point together—oh yes, don't look so surprised," Arthur Doyle said. "I went to West Point with Rufus. I was a good student, too, Rufus' equal, I believe, intellectually, but never physically. I simply did not have the physical attributes to be a good officer."

"It doesn't take physical attributes to command men, Mr. Doyle," O'Grady said, "but you know that."

"Yes, of course I do," Doyle said, "but you know

as well as I that what men judge other men by initially is their appearance. Do you deny judging me by mine, the other night?"

"No, sir," O'Grady said, "I don't, but I was wrong, obviously."

Doyle waved away O'Grady's apology, if that's what it was.

"The army life was not for me, anyway," Doyle said. "I soon learned that. So I went into business and have done quite well for myself."

"Obviously."

"It was at the Point, though, where Rufus and I first met Lia, my wife, Anja's mother." A faraway look came into Doyle's eyes as he spoke of his wife. "She was beautiful, and we both fell in love with her. I thought I had no chance with her, but a strange thing happened. She fell in love with *me*, not Rufus, and when I left the Point we married." Doyle came back to the present and looked at O'Grady. "Rufus Wheeler has never forgiven me for that, as he has never forgiven me for her death."

"Her death?"

"We were married twenty-five years ago," Doyle said, "and my daughter is nineteen. Lia became pregnant three times before Anja was born, and lost the baby all three times. Each miscarriage left her weaker than the last, but we—I—insisted on trying again . . . and again . . . and again. Finally, Anja was born—and my wife died in childbirth. For that Rufus has hated me for nineteen years—as I have hated myself."

"Sir?"

"It was my pigheaded stubbornness to have a son that ultimately killed my wife, Mr. O'Grady," Doyle said. "Now I have no son, and no wife. I have only my daughter, and I am putting her life into your hands."

O'Grady hesitated a moment before saying, "I understand, sir."

"Save her, Mr. O'Grady," Doyle said. "Please save her."

O'Grady stood up and said, "I'll bring her back, Mr. Doyle."

Doyle nodded and drifted off again into thought. O'Grady didn't know at what time in the past Doyle's mind had wandered, but he left him there and took his leave.

In the entry lobby, he came across the black man, who opened the door for him.

"What's your name?" he asked the man.

"Henry, sir."

"Henry," O'Grady said, "I believe Mr. Doyle might want some coffee—or something stronger."

"Yes, sir," Henry said, "I'll see to it."

O'Grady nodded and started out the door.

"Mr. O'Grady?" Henry said.

On the porch O'Grady turned and said, "Yes?"

"You'll be bringing Miss Anja back to us, won't you, sir?"

"Yes, Henry," O'Grady said without hesitation. "I will be bringing her back."

From Doyle's house O'Grady went to the saloon where he, Preacher and Adam Shea had talked the day before. Both Preacher and Shea were there, with their grips at their side. Shea's bag was new, while Preacher's was an old and tattered carpetbag.

It was before noon, and the place was empty. In fact, it was too empty.

Preacher noticed the look on O'Grady's face and said, "I gave the bartender a few dollars to leave us alone for a while."

"Good," O'Grady said. He had already split up the

expense money after leaving Doyle's house, so he now gave them each a separate envelope with five thousand dollars inside. Neither of them took the money out, but counted it in the envelope.

Shea stared at the money, and then looked at O'Grady wonderingly.

"This is for expenses?"

"That's right."

Shea looked at Preacher and said, "Imagine what the payoff is going to be."

Preacher nodded. He didn't show it, but he *was* imagining it.

"All this just to bring back one girl?" Shea asked.

"That's the job."

"Her father must be very rich," Shea said.

O'Grady didn't reply.

A crafty look crept into Preacher's pale eyes and he said, "He must be *very* wealthy, indeed."

Again, O'Grady said nothing.

"O'Grady," Preacher said, "is this Arthur Doyle's daughter we're looking for?"

"What made you ask that?"

"I read the newspapers," Preacher said. "These was something about Anja Doyle going to Texas a month or so ago—and who else would have this kind of money to throw around?"

"He's right, isn't he?" Shea asked.

O'Grady hesitated, then decided, why not?

"All right, yes, it's Anja Doyle."

"The Mexicans must be holding her for some kind of ransom," Preacher said.

"A *big* ransom," Shea said.

O'Grady stared at Preacher and Shea and, for the first time, wondered if he was making a mistake. Would a million dollars tempt either, or both, of them? What about the others? Jinx, C.K. and Blackjack? How would a million dollars look to them?

"It doesn't make a difference whose daughter it is," O'Grady asked, "does it?"

"No—well, yes, yes it does," Shea said. "At least we know now that there really *is* a pot of gold at the end of the rainbow."

"You fellas better get going," O'Grady said, "or you're going to miss your train."

"Right," Shea said.

He and Preacher put their money away inside their jackets and stood up.

"We'll see you in Medallion in ten days or so," Preacher said.

"Right."

O'Grady let Preacher and Shea leave first, but first asked Preacher to recommend another hotel where he could spend the night. He had no intentions of going back to the Denver House.

"It's not going to be as pretty as where you are," Preacher warned him.

"I'm not worried about that."

Preacher nodded and gave him the location of a hotel.

"Tell them I sent you."

O'Grady nodded, and watched the two men leave. He gave them five minutes and then stood up and left himself. He wasn't worried about the police having followed him there. There was likely only one man on him, and he would *stay* on him, so no one would be following Preacher and Shea to the train station. All the policeman would know was that O'Grady had met with two men and handed them something. Let Inspector Names make of that what he could.

*   *   *

From the saloon he went to the livery where he had placed Cormac upon arriving in Denver and made sure that the animal would be ready to travel when Doyle's man came for him. He paid his bill, spent a few minutes with the horse, and then left. After the livery he went to the hospital, in spite of Wheeler's having told him to stay away.

Both Sister Madrid and Sister Marie were at the front desk.

"Hello, Mr. O'Grady," the older nun said. Sister Marie just smiled at him. Nuns shouldn't be that pretty, he thought.

"Hello, Sisters," O'Grady said. "How is the patient?"

"Oh," Sister Madrid said, rolling her eyes, "a *terrible* patient."

"An *im*patient patient," Sister Maria said, and laughed at her own joke.

"And his condition?"

"Stable," Sister Madrid said. "He won't be leaving the hospital for a while, but he is in no danger."

"Is there still a policeman on his door?"

"Yes," Sister Madrid said, "A different one every four hours."

"Has Inspector Names been back to see him?"

"Oh, yes," she said, "several times."

"Now *there* is an impatient man," Sister Marie said, and Sister Madrid nodded her agreement.

"Every time he leaves he seems annoyed about something," she said, shaking her head. "How could that poor man help it if someone shot him. The inspector acts like it's Mr. Wheeler's own fault."

"Do you wish to see him?" Sister Marie asked.

"If I can, yes."

She smiled and said, "I will walk you back."

"Thank you, Sister."

Instead of following her—since he already knew the way—he walked alongside of her.

"Excuse me for asking, Sister Marie," O'Grady said, "but you seem very young. Have you taken your final vows yet?"

"Why yes, I have," she said. "Why do you ask?"

"No reason," he said. "Just curious."

Sister Marie managed to get him past the policeman on the door and Wheeler looked much as he had the other times he had been there.

"What are you doing here now?" the man asked. His mood had obviously not improved.

"Keeping you up to date on what's happening," O'Grady said.

"Good," Wheeler said, "it'll take my mind off my— go ahead. What's going on?"

O'Grady told Wheeler what he was planning to do, when he was leaving, where he was going, and about his conversations with Inspector Names. He did *not* tell him about his talk with Arthur Doyle.

"The inspector is going to be livid when he finds out I've left," he finished.

"Leave him to me," Wheeler said. "I'll handle him. You just do what you have to do to save that girl."

"Yes, sir."

"And make sure you don't give any money to Fuljencio," Wheeler added. "Is that totally understood?"

"Yes, sir."

"I mean it, O'Grady," Wheeler said. "Even if it looks like the only way to get the girl out, don't let that Mexican bandido get his hands on any U.S. money."

"I understand, sir."

Wheeler frowned and said, "When you start yessing me, I worry."

"Don't worry, sir," O'Grady said. "Everything will go fine."

O'Grady decided to tell Wheeler what he had found out about the shooter.

"The nerve of the man!" Wheeler snapped. "Shooting me from my own room."

"I don't know if the police are aware of it or not," O'Grady said, "but if I tell them—"

"Don't," Wheeler said. "I told you to stay out of it."

"Yes, sir."

"I'll try and arrange it so they find out on their own," Wheeler said. "Now get out of here. I don't want to see you again until you get back. In fact, I don't want to see you here at all. I'll be going back to Washington as soon as I can. I will see you *there* when this is all over."

"Yes, sir."

"We're counting on you, O'Grady."

"I know, sir."

"Good luck."

O'Grady paused at the door, looked back at the man in the bed and said, "You, too, sir."

When he got back to the front desk, he asked Sister Madrid, "Sister, is there a side door to the hospital?"

"Side, and back," she said. "Are you avoiding someone out front?"

"I'm afraid I am, Sister," O'Grady said.

She nodded knowingly and said to Sister Marie, "Sister, will you show Mr. O'Grady another way out?"

"It would be my pleasure," the younger nun said. "This way, Mr. O'Grady."

Even though he knew he'd never see her again, O'Grady said to her, "Call me Canyon, Sister."

12

Preacher O'Mara and Adam Shea sat in the saloon in Medallion, Texas, looking across the room at the only other men seated in the saloon.

"It's got to be them," Adam Shea said. "Who the hell else could they be waiting for?"

"They could be waiting for anyone," Preacher said. "That's what this place is for, to wait."

Preacher had already explained to Shea that Medallion was a sort of way station for anyone who was traveling from Texas into Mexico. The general store did a brisk business with anyone who was stocking up for the ride south of the border. The hotel also did a good business with people stopping overnight, or even longer—as they were doing. And as the other two men were obviously doing, as well.

Of course, Shea was right. The other two men in the room had to be Blackjack Decker and C.K. Fletcher. How or why they came to be here together was not Preacher's concern. He and Shea had been told not to approach anyone, and since Preacher had agreed to work for O'Grady, that meant that he would do what O'Grady said.

"Where's the harm in just walking over and askin' them," Shea wondered aloud.

"No," Preacher said.

"Why not?"

"Because O'Grady said not to."

"We got to do everything he says?"

"Yes."

"Preacher," Shea said, "I didn't think you were afraid of anyone."

"I'm not afraid of O'Grady," Preacher said. "I respect him."

"So why do we have to do everything he says?" Shea asked.

"Because we've agreed to work for him," Preacher said, "and when you agree to work for someone, you do what he says. It is the same way with my agreement to work for the Lord, and to spread his word."

"Oh, Christ," Shea said, "you ain't gonna start talkin' to me about God, are you?"

"You are a heathen," Preacher said, "I would never speak with you about our Lord, Jesus Christ. However, if you continue to take his name in vain, I will have to reprimand you."

Shea looked across the table at Preacher, whose pale eyes were not looking his way. For this he was grateful. He *hated* when Preacher turned those eyes his way. Preacher may not have been afraid of Canyon O'Grady, but Adam Shea was certainly afraid of Preacher O'Mara. Shea was not really here in reply to O'Grady's request. He was here because Preacher had come for him and said they had a job of work to do, and Shea never turned Preacher down.

Never.

Of course, he'd die before he'd ever admit that to anyone, hence his usual blustery front.

"Sure, Preacher," Shea said, "whatever you say . . . I just don't see the *harm* of talking to them."

"There is no harm," Preacher said. "We are just not going to do it."

"Well, how long are we gonna wait?" Shea asked.

"I mean, O'Grady was supposed to be a day behind us, and this is our second day here."

"We'll wait," Preacher said, "as long as we have to wait until he gets here."

"Yeah, well . . ." Shea said, and stared into his empty beer mug.

On the other side of the room the other two men—who were, of course, Blackjack Decker and C.K. Fletcher—were wondering the same things about Preacher and Shea.

"I'd swear that's Preacher O'Mara," Blackjack Decker said.

"Why?" Fletcher asked. "Who's he?"

"You've never heard of O'Mara, the Preacher?" Decker asked.

"No, I ain't," Fletcher said, "so what? Who is he?"

"He's a Preacher who's just about the best hand with a gun I ever—well, I've never *seen* him, but I've heard of him."

"What makes you think it's him?" Fletcher asked.

"Well, the dark hair and the white hair," Decker said. "He sure *looks* like the descriptions I've heard of Preacher O'Mara."

"So why don't we go over and ask him?" Fletcher said. "I mean, if he's such a hero of yours."

"He's not a hero," Decker said, "he's a legend. It's a different thing."

"Legends are just guys who are old," Fletcher said.

"I tell you what." Decker said. "Why don't you go over there and tell him that?"

Fletcher moved around in his chair nervously and said, "Hey, I'm not the one who's curious about the guy."

"Then shut up," Decker said. "We'll just sit here

and wait for O'Grady to show up, and then we'll find out what's going on."

"They must be waiting for O'Grady, too," Fletcher said. "Why else would they be sittin' here?"

"Like I said," Decker said, "we'll wait for O'Grady to arrive and then we'll find out."

O'Grady rode into Medallion and went directly to the livery, where he turned Cormac over to a sleepy liveryman. While he was there he was pleased to see the other horses inside the livery.

From here he went to the hotel and got himself a room. In Medallion there was no need to register at the hotel; you simply walked in and got a key. Because of that there was no register book for O'Grady to read and see if Preacher, Shea and the others actually were present in town. He knew where he could go, however, to find that out, so he left his gear in his hotel and walked over to the saloon.

When O'Grady walked into the saloon he went directly to the bar, ordered five beers, and then with the bartender's help carried them to a table right in the center of the room.

"All right," he said, "I guess you guys might as well come over here and sit together. We have a lot of planning to do."

"I said you guys were here to meet with O'Grady," C.K. Fletcher said. "Didn't I say that, Deck? I said that to Decker. I said you guys were here to see O'Grady."

"I guess that makes you pretty smart, kid," Adam Shea said.

Fletcher glared at Shea, wondering if the man was making fun of him.

"I knew you were Preacher O'Mara," Blackjack Decker said when they finally sat together. "I've heard a lot about you, Preacher. It's going to be interesting to see if everything I've heard about you is true."

Preacher, without looking directly at Decker, said, "I hope you're not disappointed." He looked at O'Grady and asked, "I thought you said there was going to be six of us?"

"Six?" Decker asked. "Who's the sixth?"

"Jinx Quinones."

"Who?" Fletcher asked.

"I know Jinx," Decker said.

"What's a Jinx?" Fletcher asked.

"I still don't see a woman being involved in this," Adam Shea said.

"A woman?" Fletcher asked. "Jinx is a woman?"

"You know what a woman looks like, kid?" Shea asked, with a grin.

"Don't call me kid," Fletcher said to Shea. "I don't like it."

"Sure, kid."

"Hey—"

"Jinx will pull her own weight," O'Grady said, cutting Fletcher off, "don't worry about that."

"I know Jinx," Decker said. "She can handle herself fine . . . but what is it we're getting involved in here, O'Grady?"

"We could wait for Jinx so I don't have to say this twice," O'Grady said, "but I guess I'll just go ahead and lay it out for you. Preacher, you and Shea already know all this, so just be patient."

O'Grady laid it out all very carefully for Decker and Fletcher. He told them what had happened in Denver, although he never mentioned Rufus Wheeler's name.

He simply told them that there had been some shooting in Denver, which may or may not have been involved with their job.

After O'Grady finished talking, Blackjack Decker said, "This sounds like fun."

"Fun?" C.K. Fletcher said. "It sounds like suicide to me."

"Hey, kid, you and I agree on something," Shea said. "How about that?"

"I told you not to call me kid."

"Settle down," O'Grady said. "Let's find out who's in and who's out." He looked at Decker.

"Oh, I'm in," Decker said, "definitely in."

"Fletcher?"

"Maybe he should ask permission from his mother," Shea suggested.

"Hey, you—" Fletcher started, but O'Grady interrupted him again, this time to speak to Shea.

"Shut up, Shea," he said, and then looked at Fletcher again. "Fletch?"

"I'm in, O'Grady," Fletcher said, glaring at Shea. "Preacher?"

"Still in," Preacher said. "I did not come all this way to pull out."

"Neither did I," Shea said.

"Good," O'Grady said. "Now that we're all in, we've got other things to discuss. Preacher, what about supplies?"

"I've got most of what we need. Now that I know there will be . . . six of us?"

"Six," O'Grady said, sure that Jinx would show up.

"Six of us," Preacher said, "I'll have to pick up a few things."

"Okay," O'Grady said. "Shea, what about the explosives?"

"I've got everything we need," Shea said, "which is

good. I doubt I could get anything I need in this one-horse town."

"You'd be surprised what you can get in Medallion," O'Grady said. "Deck, why don't you check with everybody on weapons. I want to know what we have to work with."

"I'll take care of it."

"Fletch, you check on everyone's horses. I want to make sure before we start that everybody's got enough horse under them."

"Right."

"Let's go, then."

Preacher, Decker and Fletcher got up and left the saloon and Shea turned to O'Grady and said, "What do you want me to do?"

"I want you to stop picking on the kid," O'Grady said.

"Ah, I can handle the kid."

"I'm not worrying about you handling the kid."

"Why, you don't think I can?"

"Let's just say I wouldn't put any money on it," O'Grady said. "Why don't you just go and find yourself a woman and stay under the sheets for a while?"

"That's just what I'll do," Shea said, and stormed out of the saloon.

O'Grady sat in the saloon alone, wondering if mixing and matching these distinct personalities was such a good idea, after all. Of course, it was too late to worry about that now. They had a job to do, and he intended to see that it got done.

He had thought a lot about the job during his trip from Denver to Texas. He had promised Arthur Doyle that he would never deliberately do anything to endanger his daughter's life, but wasn't that just what he was doing? In his pocket right at that moment was a bank draft for a million dollars. If his intention had been to actually pay the ransom, he would have cashed the draft as soon as he arrived in Texas. Since he didn't have any intention of paying that money to General Fuljencio, wasn't that just what he was doing? And yet he could see Rufus Wheeler's point in not letting any of that money fall into the hands of the would-be *presidente* of Mexico. It certainly wouldn't look good if anyone ever found out that American money funded an overthrow of the Mexican government—or *any* government. The American government would *never* fund the overthrow of a foreign government, never in a hundred years.

Would they?

13

Jinx Quinones knew she should not be riding to Medallion, Texas, to meet Canyon O'Grady. The man *infuriated* her. He *always* made her mad, and she knew that. Take, for instance, his message to her to meet him in Medallion. No explanation, there was not even the hint of a request in the message. O'Grady *assumed* that she would respond to his summons—and here she was, doing it. Sometimes she just infuriated herself.

On the other hand, Canyon O'Grady was the most beautiful man she had ever known. She had never had sex with any man that matched the sex she had with O'Grady. Jesus, Canyon O'Grady was the only man who could make her cry during sex. He actually made her *weep*.

He was also exciting. The times she had worked with him, he always got her involved in something exciting—aside from being an exciting man himself.

Just riding towards Medallion to meet with him, to *be* with him, she felt herself growing excited—and *that* infuriated her.

But she kept riding.

O'Grady was sitting in a chair outside the saloon when Preacher O'Mara came walking over.

"Think she's coming?" Preacher asked.

"She's coming," O'Grady said.

"You seem pretty sure."

O'Grady looked at Preacher and said, "Of all of you, she's the one I was dead sure would show up."

Preacher looked up and down the street and said, "She's not here yet."

"She likes to make me wait," O'Grady said. He looked at Preacher and said, "Got everything we need?"

"Do I need anything special for her?"

"No," O'Grady said. "She'll do and eat the same things we do."

"Then I have everything."

"I want to talk to you about Shea."

"What about him?"

"Keep a tight rein on him," O'Grady said.

"He's not my responsibility."

"I'm making him your responsibility," O'Grady said. "Keep him off Fletcher."

"Oh," Preacher said, "that."

"Yeah, that. Why's he got it in for the kid?"

"That's Shea," Preacher said. "You know that. You knew that when you asked him in on this."

"I guess I did," O'Grady said. "I guess I forgot."

"I'll watch him."

"Thanks."

Preacher looked up the street and said, "Rider coming in."

"Uh-huh."

"Looks like a woman with long, dark hair," Preacher said. "That her?"

"That's her."

O'Grady looked up the street and saw her riding in.

"She's very beautiful," Preacher said.

"Yes, she is."

Preacher looked at O'Grady and said, "Having her on the trail with five men might cause problems."

O'Grady answered without taking his eyes off of Jinx. She was one of the most desirable women he had ever known. Just sitting a horse she stirred his juices a lot more than a lot of women in expensive gowns.

"She can handle it."

"I hope so."

O'Grady looked at Preacher and said, "Just look after Shea, Preacher."

"I'll keep an eye on him," Preacher said, "but I won't babysit him."

"Fine."

As Jinx came closer Preacher said, "I'll take a stroll around town. See you later."

"Right."

As Preacher walked away, Jinx spotted O'Grady and rode over to where he was sitting.

"That looked like Preacher O'Mara," Jinx said, looking down at him.

"It was."

She nodded and did not get down off her horse.

"Anyone else involved like him?"

"Of his caliber?" O'Grady asked. "I guess he's about the best. We've got Blackjack Decker, too."

"I know Deck."

"A couple of fellas named C.K. Fletcher and Adam Shea," he said.

She nodded, not saying if she knew who they were or not.

"And you."

"Me."

"Right."

"You sonofabitch."

"Hi, Jinx."

*　　*　　*

Jinx Quinones was the most responsive woman Canyon O'Grady had ever been to bed with. As soon as he touched her nipples tremors rolled through her body and she gasped, her mouth hanging open.

He finished undressing her and lowered her to the bed in his hotel room. He hadn't seen her in a few years, so he took the time to study her. She was tall, about five seven, with long, well-muscled legs, a slim waist, and full, well-rounded breasts with dark brown nipples. The hair between her legs was black as night and very bushy, while the hair on her head—also the blackest of black—was long and wild.

He sat next to her on the bed and rolled her over, running his hand down the line of her back, over the swell of her buttocks, which were as muscular as her legs and thighs. He leaned over and kissed her buttocks, running his tongue over the cleft between them. He kissed the back of her thighs, the hollows behind her knees, then spread her legs so he could kiss the inside of her thighs. She spread her legs very wide for him and the lower portion of her body rose up off the bed. He got behind her and lifted her up onto her knees, so that her butt was offered to him.

He slipped one hand between her legs and felt for her until he found her, hot and wet, slickly ready. He slid the middle finger of his right hand inside of her, and she gasped and leaned back against him, saying something in Spanish that he could not catch.

She started to rock back against his hand, and he removed his finger and positioned himself behind her, taking hold of her hips. His penis, long and rigid, rested on the smooth slopes of her buttocks. He slid it down between the cheeks of her ass, then lower until he could slide it past her inner thighs. She moaned and pressed back against him as the head of his penis came in contact with her moist portal. He let the head slide inside of her and the feeling was so exquisite that he impatiently thrust the rest of his length inside of her so quickly and *hard* that she grunted aloud and then let out a long moan as he started easing himself in and out of her, holding her by the hips, then quickened his tempo so that the room was filled with the sound of flesh slapping flesh, moans and cries from both of them, little screams as he reached underneath to grasp her hanging breasts, pinch her nipples, as he began to slam into her so hard that the bed would take little hops and jumps across the floor . . .

"Oh, dios mio . . ." Jinx said later.

He was between her thighs again, but in the more customary missionary position, so that he could look down at her face as he drove into her, or lean over and lick and kiss her breasts . . .

"Oh, madre de dios . . ." Jinx cried out, bringing her powerful thighs up to wrap them around his lean waist, groping at his back with her hands, raking him with her nails, and then the tears began to roll down her cheeks.

She had cried before, when she was on her knees, but from behind her he could not see it. Now that they were face-to-face he saw the tears streaming down her face, and he knew that she was crying from pure pleasure . . .

Still later, she said to him, "Damn you, Canyon O'Grady, you are the only man who can make me cry."

They were dressing and he turned to look at her. He was in time to see her pull her pants up over her

96

lovely butt, and he felt the loss as her beautiful ass was hidden from view.

"I'm glad you came, Jinx," he said.

"You knew I would come," she said, her back still to him. "That is one of the things about you that makes me so angry."

"And there are many."

"There are *very* many," she said.

She finished dressing and reached for her gunbelt, which was on the bedpost. His gun was hanging on the other bedpost. They both strapped them on and then looked at each other.

"Let's get away from this bed," she said, "so I can think straight, and you can explain to me *why* you sent for me."

14

O'Grady took Jinx down to the saloon to explain the job to her.

"Get me another beer," she said, when he was finished.

He got up, got her a beer from the bar and brought it back to the table, along with one more for himself.

"This is crazy," she said.

"No it's not."

"Six people cannot take on a whole army."

"That's not what we're doing," O'Grady said. "We're not going to try and defeat Fuljencio's army. We're only going to try and get the girl away from him."

"It's the same thing."

"There's a lot of money in this, Jinx."

"For who?"

"For you, and the others."

"And not you?"

"I'm doing it for different reasons."

"Like what? Do you know this girl? This woman?"

"No, it's nothing like that."

"Then what?"

"You're asking too many questions, now."

O'Grady had worked with all of these people before, but none of them knew that he was an agent for the United States government, and it would stay that way.

"The others have agreed?" she asked.

"Yes."

"Preacher? Decker?"

"And the other two."

"Who are they?"

Briefly, he told her who Fletcher and Shea were.

"Can they be trusted?"

"When it comes time for the action," he said, "yes. You'll meet them all tonight."

"But I must agree first."

"Yes."

"How much money am I likely to see out of this?" she asked.

He told her, and she was impressed.

"That is a lot of money," she said.

"Yes."

"And all I have to do to get it is get this girl out of Mexico, and live to collect it."

"That's all."

She shook her head and said to herself, "Madness."

"Does that means that the answer is yes?" he asked.

She looked at him and said, "Yes, damn you, the answer *is* yes."

They gathered that evening in the saloon and, although there were other patrons there, they were able to secure a back table where they wouldn't be disturbed.

The first thing O'Grady did was make all the proper introductions.

"Well," Adam Shea said, staring in open admiration at Jinx, "you were certainly worth waiting for."

"I would like to get something straight before we begin," Jinx said, ignoring him.

"I'm all ears," Shea said, smiling.

"Until we are finished with this . . . job . . . I will consider myself one of you."

"I like the way this sounds," Shea said.

"That means that we will eat the same things, sleep in the same places, and I will share evenly whatever chores we face."

"Gettin' better all the time," Shea said.

"What it does not mean," Jinx went on, "is that I am the community whore. The first man who tries to touch me in that way, or who continues to make remarks to me, will find himself gelded." She took out her knife, which had a shiny, finely honed edge, and looked directly at Adam Shea. "Do I make myself clear?"

Shea stared at the knife, and then looked away.

"Very clear," Preacher said. Somewhat mollified, Jinx put her knife away and looked at O'Grady.

"Can we get on with this, now?" Preacher asked O'Grady. "I assume we are here so that you can tell us what fine strategy you have come up with."

"There's not much in the way of strategy that we can come up with until we know exactly what we're up against," O'Grady said. "We don't know where Fuljencio and his army are, and we don't really know how many men he has, although we do have some idea."

"What *do* we know, then?" Jinx asked.

"We know where the ransom is to be paid."

"Where?" she asked.

"A small village called Malo."

"Where is it?" Preacher asked.

"We have directions," O'Grady said. He had written out a set for each of them to look at. "From the looks of them, it's off the beaten path."

"Mexico is off the beaten path," Shea said, sourly. He hadn't looked at Jinx since she put her knife away.

"They wouldn't want to meet anywhere the *federales* might stumble upon by accident," Preacher said.

"Is Fuljencio going to make the pickup himself?" Decker asked.

"That I don't know," O'Grady said.

"You're just supposed to hand the money over to the first person who asks for it?" Preacher asked.

"I'm to ride into Malo and wait," O'Grady said. "Those are my instructions."

"Alone," Jinx said, flicking the piece of paper in her right hand with her left index finger, "you're supposed to ride in alone. How are you going to explain the rest of us being along?"

"I'm not," O'Grady said. "You'll be the only one who rides in with me, Jinx."

Jinx smiled and said, "I am to be the *duena*?" The chaperone.

"That's right."

"How quaint."

"And the rest of us?" Decker asked.

"Deck, I want you and C.K. to ride ahead," O'Grady said. "Preacher and Shea will ride behind us."

"Cover your back," Preacher said.

"Right."

"How do you want C.K. and me to play it?"

O'Grady looked at Fletcher and asked, "Can you speak Spanish?"

"Not a word."

"I can," Decker said.

"I know that," O'Grady said. "Deck, do you think Fletch can pass for Mexican, if he keeps his mouth shut?"

Decker looked at Fletcher and said, "Maybe, but how do you plan to keep his mouth shut?"

"That's easy," O'Grady said. "We'll cut out his tongue."

"What?"

As it turned out, Fletcher—much to his pleasure—was only to *figuratively* have his tongue cut out, in that he would be playing the part of a mute. Decker, utilizing his considerable talents as a con man, would be able to pass for Mexican under the most ardent of tests.

Decker and Fletcher, then, would ride into Malo several days ahead of O'Grady and Jinx. One of the reasons O'Grady was taking Jinx with him was that she could speak Spanish. Preacher could also speak it, so pairing him with Shea—who could not—made sense. O'Grady also wanted to keep Shea away from Fletcher *and* Jinx, both of whom he had managed to alienate. That made the pairings fairly simple and logical.

"Can I ask a question?" Jinx said.

"Go ahead."

"Where is the ransom money?"

"I don't have it."

"Why not?" Jinx asked. "I mean, why aren't we just paying the ransom and taking her home?"

"Two reasons," O'Grady said. "If we pay them a million dollars, they'll use it to fund their revolution. A lot of people will get killed because of that money."

"Maybe they won't," Shea said.

"What?"

"Maybe once this guy Fuljencio has the money he'll decide that he'd rather keep it than use it to become president of Mexico."

"That's a possibility," O'Grady said, "but not one we can count on."

"What's the other reason?" Jinx asked.

"Once I pay him the ransom," O'Grady said, "he'd probably kill her—*and* me—anyway."

After the meeting Decker and Fletcher remained in the saloon. Preacher and Shea left and separated outside. O'Grady and Jinx left together, and saw Preacher and Shea walking in opposite directions.

"Are those two friends?" she asked.

"It's hard to explain what those two are," he said.

"A man of God who carries a gun," she said, shaking her head. "I have heard of him, but thought he was a myth."

"He's no myth."

"And the other one," she said, "seems intent on getting himself killed."

"One way or another," he said. When she looked at him he said, "Shea's specialty is explosives."

"Ah," she said, "so he *enjoys* living dangerously, then."

"I guess so."

"But then don't we all?"

O'Grady shrugged and said, "Some of us don't do it because we enjoy it."

"That is true," she said. "Some of us are compelled to do the things we do."

They both knew that she was talking about their afternoon together.

"Jinx—"

"I am going to bed, O'Grady," she said, "in my room, alone. Good night."

"Good night."

He watched her walk away and knew that she was as big an enigma as the others were. Decker enjoyed *being* somebody else, fleecing someone else out of their money, or simply being himself and *winning* someone's money across a poker table. Either of those was a dangerous way to make a living. And Fletcher—well, C.K. Fletcher was young, and that in itself was dangerous.

Canyon O'Grady did what he did because he felt he had to. There was no enjoyment, there was no compulsion. That he *had* to do what he did had nothing to do with being *compelled* to do it. In most circumstances he did what he did for his country. In a way, some of this was for that reason, but there was also the life of a young woman at stake.

15

General Fernando Maximilan Fuljencio reached up to grasp the full, heavy breasts of the woman who was straddling him. Her name was Estralita, and it was her duty to pleasure her leader whenever he craved it—which was often. Luckily, Estralita was not the only young woman in Fuljencio's camp with the same duty. The general was insatiable, and it took more than one woman to see to his pleasures.

Luckily for Estralita she was *also* in the mood at the moment, so she was enjoying the feel of the general's huge penis filling her, and also his rough handling of her breasts. He pawed her flesh, grasped her hard enough to leave bruises, brutalized her nipples with his fingers, then reached for her and pulled her down so that he could bite them.

He grabbed a handful of her wild black hair and pulled her face to his, mashing her lips with his, thrusting his tongue into her mouth. This she did not like, because the general had foul breath and tasted of cheap cigars and even cheaper whiskey. When he released her she sat back up on him and began to ride him more quickly, anxious now to end their liaison. The general, however, had a reputation among women as being a man who could go on forever, and at the moment he was living up to that reputation.

Finally he threw her off of him, set her up on her

hands and knees and roughly entered her from behind. She knew that he always did this when he was ready to finish. As he slammed into her she cried out, in both pain *and* pleasure, but the general was oblivious to her. He only knew the pounding need in his own loins. He grasped her hips tightly and pulled her back toward him as he plunged into her, over and over again, mindlessly. Finally he bellowed like a wounded bull and exploded into her, and then tossed her aside to the hard-packed ground, where she waited, watching him, hoping that he would not want her again so soon. Her own need had been more than satisfied and she now wanted nothing more than to go off and rest, for she knew she would be very sore later.

Fuljencio, who always seemed to be in a trance during sex, stared at her with unseeing eyes, and then slowly his eyes began to focus. When he realized that she was still there he would either take her again, or tell her to leave. She held her breath and waited.

"Go!" he finally said, and she got quickly to her feet, grabbed her dress and ran naked from his tent. From outside the general could hear the laughter of his men, and of some of the women, and he smiled, and then laughed out loud.

He sat on the edge of his bed, which he had brought out here from Mexico City, and scratched his balls. His penis responded to his own touch, thickening slightly.

"Enough, my friend," he said, speaking to it as if it was alive, "there are other pleasures in life to be enjoyed, no?"

He reached out and grabbed one of his cheap cigars. For a man who enjoyed a soft, expensive bed, his taste in cigars was terrible, and yet he enjoyed drawing the acrid, foul-smelling smoke into his lungs and then expelling the almost blue smoke into the air around him.

Fuljencio stood up, and his balls hung heavily between his legs, as did his penis. Again, he reached down and scratched himself. He was forty-five, over six feet tall, built like a bull, thick through the waist and chest, with legs and thighs like tree trunks. His entire body was covered with wiry black hair. He had a full beard and mustache, and the only place hair seemed incapable of surviving was on his head. There he had only wispy memories of hair, and those he left to fly about on their own.

"Raphael!" he shouted.

Immediately his aide, Lieutenant Raphael Gonzales entered the tent, anxious to serve his leader.

"Si, mi Generale?"

"Food."

"Chicken, *mi Generale?*"

"What else?" Fuljencio bellowed. "And make it a whole one."

"Si, mi Generale."

Fuljencio loved chicken. He loved eating them whole, tearing them apart with his hands, feeling the grease between his fingers, and on his face. Fuljencio, when it came to food and women, was a pig. He knew it, and reveled in it, because he was powerful enough to *be* a pig if he wanted to be.

When Raphael came in with his leader's chicken, Fuljencio was still naked. He enjoyed displaying his nakedness to his men, because he was proud of the size of his genitals. He knew that women desired him, and that men felt dwarfed by him.

He dined on the chicken and wine, and then called Raphael in again. He was wiping his greasy hands in his pubic hair when the man entered. The next whore he had would have chicken grease for dessert.

"Bring the girl in," he told Raphael.

"*Si, mi Generale,*" Raphael said. He removed the remnants of the chicken and backed out of the tent.

Outside Raphael said to one of the men, a corporal, "Bring the girl."

"*Si, Teniente,*" the man said, and went off to get the girl.

Outside of the general's tent, Raphael was in command. Once he entered the tent, he was like the other men, dwarfed by the general's size, the booming voice, the arrogance of the man. Most of the general's men were afraid of him. The only man who was *not* afraid of him was *Capitan* Roberto Colon Velez Salazar. Salazar was perhaps the only man alive who Raphael admired. He was tall, and handsome, and was not intimidated by General Fuljencio, Raphael could not understand the relationship the two men had, but Fuljencio and Salazar seemed to genuinely be friends. It was puzzling, indeed.

The corporal brought the *gringa* and Raphael took her by the arm. He admired this *gringa*, too. She was beautiful, and she was brave. She never showed fear to the general no matter how he tried to terrify her.

"Inside," he said, gruffly, pushing her ahead of him.

As they entered the tent he saw that the general had not covered his nakedness. He watched the girl's face, and although her eyes widened slightly at the size of the general's manhood, she showed no other sign of fear.

Fuljencio stood with his feet spread, his hands on his hips, giving the *gringa* a good look at him. He knew that he had been unable to make her show fear, but maybe he could force her into a display of desire. Yes, she *was* looking at him. Was that desire he saw in her face? In the heaving of her breasts?

"Out, Raphael," the general said, and Raphael backed out without a word.

"So, *chica*," the general said, "what do you think of your general, eh?"

Anja Doyle looked him straight in the eye for a moment, then looked down at the man's genitals and said, "Does that come in adult size?"

The general's eyes widened and for a moment Anja thought she may have gone too far. She and the general had been playing this game since she had first been brought here. He kept trying to frighten her and she—though terrified beyond belief—refused to show it. This was the first time he had tried to impress her with his manhood.

Had she gone too far?

She held her breath and waited.

Finally, the general threw his head back and laughed, long and hard. While laughing he reached for a pair of pants and pulled them on, covering his nakedness. She was grateful for that. She had been with only a few men, and none of them had possessed the equal to the monster the general had between his legs.

"Chica," he said, shaking his head, "you are an amazing young woman. Where do you muster this courage from?"

"I am an American."

"Oh," he said, "and all Americans are this brave? I think not."

"May I sit?" she asked.

"Si, si, sit," he said, "please."

She looked around for a chair, found one and sat. She couldn't understand the general. From the way he treated his own men—and women—he was by nature a brutal man, and yet he had not laid a hand on her, nor had he allowed anyone else to touch her.

The general sat on his expensive bed.

"Do you see this bed? I stole this from a rich man in Mexico City. It is a fine bed, no?"

"It is a very fine bed," she said.

"Have you slept well since your arrival here?"

"I have not slept well at all."

"Would you like to sleep in this bed?" he asked, patting it with one huge hand. He had gigantic hands with fingers like sausages.

"Yes," she answered, truthfully.

"With your *general*?"

"No."

He laughed again, shaking his head.

"When all others fear me, why do you not?" he asked.

"All others don't fear you."

"Oh? Name of man or woman in my camp who does *not* fear me?"

"Roberto Salazar."

The general's face turned serious.

"Ah, yes, Roberto," he said, "my friend. You admire him, eh?"

"Yes."

"And yet he serves me, who you hate."

"I don't hate you," she said, "you disgust me."

"Ah, but Roberto, he does not disgust you, eh?"

"No," she said, "he's a gentleman."

"Ah, and you like gentle men, eh?"

"Yes."

"And yet, if I told Roberto to rape you, he would do this."

"He wouldn't."

He showed her one sausagelike finger, wagged it and said, "Ah, little one, do not dare me to put this to the test."

She opened her mouth to reply, and then thought better of it. The relationship between General Fuljencio and Captain Salazar puzzled her as much as it puzzled Raphael, and many of the others in camp. One would never think that a man like Salazar would serve a man like Fuljencio—unless it was for his own reasons. She wondered what those reasons could be.

"I see you will not dare me," Fuljencio said. "*Bueno*, you are smart."

"When will you release me."

"I will release you when the money is paid," he said. "The million American dollars."

"And when is that to be?"

"Five days from now, little one," the general said, "you must suffer my company for only five more days. That pleases you, eh?"

"Very much."

"Ah, I wish I could find a Mexican woman with your fire, your courage," he said.

She didn't reply. She didn't like when he started to talk like that. She was afraid that the general liked her too much, and that he might decide to keep her— or to *use* her before he set her free.

She didn't know which would be worse.

The general had Anja taken back to her cave, where she had spent countless nights and days already. She didn't really know how long she had been there, and she didn't know if she could stand five more days without going crazy.

She looked down at her hands, which had once been so lovely—long, slender fingers with carefully tended nails. Now the nails were broken off and jagged, and her hands were filthy and chapped. She had long, auburn hair which she knew was now filthy, and her face—which had once been pretty, with soft skin—was something she was glad she could not see.

She was still wearing the riding clothes she had been

wearing the day she'd been kidnapped, but there was very little left of them. The trousers had no knees left, the sleeves were gone from her shirt. That had happened the first day she'd been brought to camp. The men had surrounded her, shunted her about, torn her clothes, until Roberto had stopped them.

Roberto.

That was the single most difficult thing to understand about this whole mess. Here was a man who she thought she could have loved, had they met under different circumstances. He rescued her from the general's men that first day, and had come to see her every day since then. He made sure she had enough to eat, he offered her clean clothes—which she refused—and he was, she thought, the reason that she had not been raped long before now.

Roberto.

He was tall, young, handsome . . . what was he doing here, serving a man who was his exact opposite? Could he really have thought that General Fernando Fuljencio *should* be the next president of Mexico?

That couldn't be. He must have had other reasons for doing what he was doing.

What could they be?

When Captain Roberto Salazar rode back into camp, he dismounted and gave his horse to one of Fuljencio's farmers. All of the farmers were given the rank of private, but Salazar always thought of them as farmers. There were forty men in camp who were trained soldiers; the rest were farmers and bandits who wanted to serve the next president of Mexico.

Salazar went to his tent and removed his saber and gun. He and Fuljencio were the only ones who had their own private quarters. Of course, he did not have a fine bed like Fuljencio, but that was all right. He slept fine on the wood and straw pallet he had.

He sat on the pallet now and thought about the two people who had been filling his thoughts lately.

Fernando Maximilan Fuljencio and Roberto Salazar were friends. It was a wary friendship, built upon mutual respect. Salazar knew how Fuljencio appeared to others. Brash, arrogant, disheveled, piggish, he was all of those things. He was also brilliant—as a soldier. Salazar was not sure what kind of president Fuljencio would make, but as a soldier he had no peer. Given enough men and enough money, Salazar was sure that Fuljencio would be able to overthrow the existing regime in Mexico and place himself in the Presidential Palace in Mexico City. That was why Salazar—who had known Fuljencio since he was a child—served him. As a child, looking up to the older Fuljencio as a little brother might to a big brother, Roberto had wanted to be like him. As he grew he realized that he *not* want to be like him, but that he did want to serve under him. Roberto wanted to learn all he could learn from Fuljencio, for he had ambitions of his own.

The other person he had been thinking a lot about these days was the *gringa* woman, Anja Doyle. From the moment he first saw her he loved her. He rescued her from Fuljencio's men that first day, and then made sure that Fernando knew that if she was harmed, he would leave.

"You want this *gringa*, Roberto?" Fuljencio had asked.

"I do not want her harmed."

"Then she will not be," Fuljencio had said, spreading his arms in an expansive gesture, "but I *will* try to frighten her a little, eh? Just to have some fun? You do not object to that, surely."

"Just do not harm her."

"Done!"

Never had he seen a woman of such a combination of beauty and courage. He *knew* that she was frightened, and yet she never showed it. Now, in five days, they were supposed to give her back, for a million American dollars—only Roberto wasn't sure Fuljencio *was* going to give her back. He didn't know *what* Fernando was going to do with her, and he was worried about it.

He decided to go and see her and make sure she was all right.

16

It was the morning after Jinx Quinones arrived that O'Grady saw Blackjack Decker and C.K. Fletcher off. Decker had purchased the proper clothing for the two of them, consisting mainly of sombreros and serapes, and Fletcher was advised to start practicing being mute right from that very moment on.

"How do you practice being mute?" he asked O'Grady and Decker.

"You don't talk," O'Grady said.

"But—"

"At all."

"But—"

"Ever!"

Fletcher looked at Decker, who just shrugged and said, *"No comprendo."*

"Be careful," O'Grady said. "I'll see you in Malo."

Decker nodded, touched the tip of his sombrero, and turned his horse.

"See you—" Fletcher started to say, but O'Grady silenced him by putting his finger to his lips. Fletcher scowled, turned his horse and hurried after Decker.

"You think he'll make it?" Jinx asked.

"He'd better," O'Grady said. "If he opens his mouth at the wrong time, they'll both be dead."

"That would be . . . inconvenient," Jinx said.

"That's one way of putting it," O'Grady said. "We leave next."

"When?"

"We'll give them a half a day's start."

"What do we do until then?" she asked.

He looked at her and she took one step back and said, "No. I'm resisting you, you bastard. I'll go and check my gear and my horse for the trip."

"Fine," he said. "I'll see what Preacher and Shea are up to."

"Fine," she said.

"See you later."

"See you."

Half an hour later they were in his bed, in his hotel room. Jinx was down between his legs, holding his penis in both hands, cooing to it, kissing it, licking it.

"It's so damned beautiful," she said, running her tongue along the underside.

"So are you," he said.

She opened her mouth wide, took him inside and then suckled him like a kid would suck a licorice stick. She even moaned "mmmmm" the way a kid might while eating a particularly sweet piece of candy.

Her head began to bob up and down on him and he lifted his hips off the bed and reached for her head, holding her there. She got to her knees so she could bring her head up and down higher and faster, moaning aloud and sucking him wetly until he groaned and exploded, filling her mouth . . .

"I thought you were resisting me," he said.

"Bastard."

They were lying side by side on their backs, their flesh wet with perspiration. He enjoyed the way she looked like that, her perfect skin glistening. He

116

propped himself up on one elbow and licked the sweat from one breast, and then from the other while she moaned and held his head.

"You keep calling me that," O'Grady said.

"That's because that's what you are," she said, pushing his head away.

He sat up in bed and looked at her.

"You know I'll come, that's why you sent for me," she said.

"I need you," he said. "I can rely on you."

"And that's the *only* time you send for me."

"Wait a minute," he said. "Are you mad at me because I sent for you, or because I don't send for you more often?"

"I don't know," she said, sitting up and reaching for her clothes. "I haven't figured that out yet."

He stared at her back for a moment, then reached for his own clothes.

"I'd better check in with Preacher and Shea," O'Grady said. "Make sure they don't have any last-minute questions."

They both got dressed and left the hotel room together.

"This time I really will check my horse," she said.

"I'll meet you at the saloon in an hour," he said. "We'll have a decent lunch so we won't have to stop on the trail until it gets dark."

She nodded and set off for the livery. He watched her walk a couple of hundred yards, then stepped down and went to look for Preacher and Shea.

He found Preacher behind the livery finally, looking at some horses. He knew Jinx was inside, tending to her own mount.

"Looking for a new horse?" O'Grady asked.

"Don't like the gait on the other one," Preacher said. "Like the lines on this one, though."

It looked like a five, or six-year-old gelding to O'Grady, dark brown and nicely filled out.

"He'll go the distance, all right," he said, patting the horse's neck. "Where's Shea?"

"Whorehouse," Preacher said, "sinning."

"Maybe he just wants to stock up on his sin because he knows we'll be on the trail a while."

"He should be praying," Preacher said.

"Yeah, well . . ." O'Grady said, unsure how to reply to that. "You fellas all set?"

"I will be after I pay for this horse," Preacher said.

"You'll be leaving first thing in the morning."

"Right."

"Shea going to be all right, Preacher?" O'Grady asked. "It's been a while since I worked with him. Anything I should know?"

"About what?"

"He seems . . . different. On the prod. Is something wrong?"

"You'd have to ask him that," Preacher said.

O'Grady studied the man for a few moments, then decided to let the subject drop.

"All right, then . . ." he said. "I'll see you later. We'll be leaving at about three."

"Fine," Preacher said. "I'll be there to see you off."

"Okay."

O'Grady started to walk away and Preacher called out to him.

"O'Grady!"

"Yeah?" O'Grady said, turning around.

"We'll watch your back, don't worry," Preacher said.

O'Grady waved and said, "I'm not worried, Preacher," and kept walking.

A little concerned, maybe . . . but not exactly worried.

*   *   *

At three O'Grady was in the livery with Jinx, and they were saddling their horses. Most of the supplies they would need were going to be carried by Preacher and Shea. They would be the only ones who had a pack animal with them. The stores O'Grady and Jinx were carrying were divvied up equally and carried in a canvas bag by each.

They were walking their horses outside when Preacher and Shea walked up on them.

"Came to see you off," Preacher said.

Shea was looking off into the distance at something only he could see.

"Appreciate it," O'Grady said. "Everyone know what they have to do?"

"Yes," Jinx said.

"Yep," Preacher said.

Shea didn't answer.

"Shea?"

The man looked at him and for a moment O'Grady thought he was going to have to repeat the question.

"I'm fine," Shea said. "I know what has to be done."

"All right, then," O'Grady said. "With a little luck the next time we see each other we'll have the girl."

"With a *lot* of luck," Shea said.

Nobody responded to that.

O'Grady and Jinx saddled up, waved to Preacher and Shea, and rode out of Medallion.

As they rode away Preacher looked at Shea and asked, "You having second thoughts about any of this?"

Shea replied without looking at Shea.

"Nope, no second thoughts."

"Now's the time—"

"I said I didn't have any second thoughts."

"Fine," Preacher said. "I'd suggest you get some sleep tonight instead of . . . whoring all night."

"I know what I need, Preacher," Shea said. "I'll meet you here at first light."

"All right, Shea."

Shea nodded and started to walk away. Preacher almost called out to him to tell him that it wouldn't be wise for him to have to come to the whorehouse in the morning and wake him up from a drunken and debauched stupor, but decided against it.

It was probably a good move.

Outside of town, Jinx said to O'Grady. "You know, if those two aren't there when we need them we're going to be in a lot of trouble."

"They'll be there."

"You mean you're sure Preacher will be there," she said. "You're *not* so sure about Shea."

O'Grady looked at her and said, "Don't worry, Preacher will have him there."

She matched his stare for a few moments, then turned her head and looked straight ahead, shaking her head, a puzzled look on her face.

"He's an odd one."

O'Grady looked at her, then decided not to ask if she meant Preacher or Shea. The answer would probably be the same.

17

Decker got a pot of coffee going on the fire and then sat on the other side from Fletcher.

"I'll take the first watch," he said to the younger man.

"Sure."

"What's the matter, kid?" Decker asked. "Having second thoughts?"

"Ain't you, Deck?" Fletcher said. "I mean, this is a whole freakin' army we're talkin' about here."

"You heard O'Grady," Decker said. "We ain't after the army, only the girl. Let the *federales* deal with the revolutionary army of Fernando Fuljencio."

"What do you know about this Fuljencio?"

"Only what I've heard," Decker said. "That he's a brutal man who's a great military mind."

"Great," Fletcher said, "and what kind of a military mind is Canyon O'Grady."

"How many times have you worked with O'Grady, kid?" Decker asked.

"Two or three . . . three, yeah. Why?"

"I've known the man for fifteen years," Decker said. "I still don't really know what he does for a living, but I do know one thing. I'd match him up against *any* Mexican revolutionary."

"Yeah, well, I guess we're gonna see if your confidence is gonna be earned, huh?"

"Hey," Decker said, "you can turn back any time you want, kid."

"I don't want," Fletcher said, and then as an afterthought he added, "and stop callin' me kid."

In another place much the same scene was taking place, only it was Canyon O'Grady seated across the fire from Jinx Quinones.

"How much ground do you think they covered today?" Jinx asked.

"Who?"

"What do you mean who? Decker and Fletcher?"

"As much as we have, I guess, and add a half a day," he said.

"I was never really good at figures," Jinx said.

"Let's just say they're a half a day ahead of us and leave it at that," he said.

"That puts them in Mexico already."

"Right," he said. "I'll take the first watch."

"Why should you take the first watch?" she asked.

"Because it was my idea."

"Remember what I said back in town? About doing my share?"

"Relax," he said, "I'm not anxious to lose my balls. You can keep watch just as long as I do, only I'll do it first. Tomorrow night you can go first. Fair?"

She thought a moment, then said, "Fair."

He poured her a cup of coffee and handed it across the fire to her.

"Have you been in Mexico before?" she asked.

"Several times."

"I've never been there."

"Really?"

"I'm *Spanish*, remember, not Mexican."

"I'm still surprised you've never been there."

"I've never had the urge, I guess."

122

"Well, you'll see it now."

"Yeah," she said, "on the run. Do you really think we can pull this off?"

"Jinx," O'Grady said seriously, "if I didn't think we had a chance I wouldn't even try it. I'm not in a hurry to die."

That made sense to her.

"All we need to do is hit and run, get the girl and get out of there. After that we only need to beat them to the border. I don't think they'll chase us across."

"Why not? They came across to get her, didn't they?" she said.

She had a point there.

Shea saw to the animals, their horses and the pack horse, and then joined Preacher at the fire. By the light of the fire Preacher was reading his Bible.

"Do you have to do that?" Shea asked.

"Do what?" Preacher asked.

"Read that book."

Preacher looked at the cover of the book in his hand, as if to remind himself of what he was reading, and then looked at Shea.

"You should read this book, Shea. It would relax you."

"I am relaxed."

"You haven't been relaxed since we talked to O'Grady in Denver," Preacher said. "Are you going to be able to handle the explosives?"

"Hey," Shea said, "my specialty, right?"

"You just seem a bit . . . nervous these days," Preacher said.

"I'm fine," Shea said, "I'll be fine."

Preacher wondered how many years it had been that Shea had been handling explosives. Maybe too many. Maybe that was his problem.

He watched Shea's right hand while the man drank his coffee, and it seemed steady enough. He only hoped it stayed that way.

"Roberto, my friend," Fuljencio said as Robert Salazar entered his tent. "It is good to see you. Sit, drink."

Salazar poured himself a cup of wine and then turned to look at his friend. Fuljencio was naked on the bed, with one of the whores—he thought it was Claudia—on the bed with him. She, too, was naked, and one of her breasts was being fondled in his right hand. It was lucky that he *had* large hands, for Claudia had *very* large breasts.

"Shall I send for one of the other women, my friend?" Fuljencio asked.

"No," Salazar said, "that will not be necessary."

"No, of course not," Fuljencio said, "it is the *gringa* you want, eh? I do not understand you, my friend. If you want her, take her." As if to bring his point across he tightened his grip on Claudia's breast and Salazar saw the look of pain cross her face. "That is what women are for, eh? To *take!*"

"Just one of the many points we do not agree on, Fernando," Salazar said. He was the only man or woman who was permitted to call Fuljencio by his first name. Even the women were instructed that during sex they were to remember to call him *mi General*.

"A strange friendship ours, eh?" Fuljencio said. "We agree on so little, how can we be such great friends?"

"We agree on the most important thing."

"And what is that?"

Salazar raised his cup and said, "That we are great friends."

"Ah, yes," Fuljencio said, "on that we *do* agree.

Chica, a cup of wine for your *general*, eh? I wish to drink a toast with my friend."

Claudia got off the bed and padded naked to the wine pitcher. Her breasts were huge, hanging almost to her waist. She poured the general a glass of wine and brought it back to him.

The general laughed, took the cup and then took hold of one of her breasts again.

"A great beast this one, eh?"

"*Si*, Fernando," Salazar said.

"We have things to discuss?" Fuljencio asked Salazar.

"*Si.*"

"Away then, beast!" Fuljencio said to Claudia. "And put your clothes on before you leave. You will drive my men crazy."

She laughed, dressed and left the tent, still giggling.

"All right, Roberto," Fuljencio said, swinging his feet to the ground, "what is it? You have that very serious look on your face."

"The ransom."

"In five days it is to be paid," Fuljencio said, "I know that."

"Four."

"Yes, all right," Fuljencio said, "four. So?"

"I think we should send some men to Malo ahead of time."

"Why?"

"Do you think the Americans are simply going to pay the ransom and that will be the end of it?" Salazar asked.

Fuljencio stood up, grabbed a pair of dirty, grimy pants and pulled them on. He then walked to a table, from which he took a cigar and lit it. The tent quickly filled with the foul smoke, but Salazar was used to it. He simply poured himself another cup of wine.

"Roberto, my friend," Fuljencio said, "am I a foolish man?"

"No, General."

"Have I ever done anything foolish— I do not mean with women—I mean when it comes to business."

"No, General."

"Then why do you assume that I am foolish when it comes to this ransom? Of course I know the Americans will try to take the girl before they pay for her, but they will not succeed, will they?"

"No."

"Of course, they will not. I have already heard from our contacts in the United States that the American government might even become involved. I have taken steps to keep that from happening—" he said, and then frowned and added, "—although I still do not know if these steps have been successfully taken. Nevertheless, do not worry. We *will* be sending men to Malo ahead of time."

"I will take them."

"No, Roberto," Fuljencio said, "you will be taking the *gringa*. You see what a great friend I am? I am giving you a last chance to be with her."

Salazar drained his wine and set the cup down.

"More wine?" Fuljencio asked.

"No, *gracias*."

"Dine with me, then."

"No, *gracias*."

"Ah, you are right. I am a pig. *I* would not eat with me if I did not have to."

"I did not mean—"

Fuljencio laughed and threw one huge arm around Salazar's shoulders.

"I know you did not mean that, my friend. Go, eat, do whatever it is you do at night. We will talk again in the morning, eh?"

"Yes, Fernando."

"Go, take a woman, Roberto," Fuljencio said, "and send one in to me—with food."

"I will send you one, Fernando," Salazar said, "with food."

As Salazar left, Fuljencio wondered what had happened to that young man he had known who liked to enjoy life. Roberto had become a very *serious* young man, now. He was still a very good soldier, however, and that was more important.

A whore named Gina, who unlike Claudia had breasts like peaches, entered the tent, carrying a whole chicken.

"Chica," Fuljencio said, and he did not know which he should devour first, the chicken or the *chica*.

Roberto Salazar went back to his tent and lay down on his pallet. Earlier he had gone to see the *gringa*, Anja Doyle, to see how she was, but she would not speak to him. He *knew*, though, that she was attracted to him, just as he was to her. He knew that, at a different time, in a different place, they might have been . . . what? Friends? Lovers? What were they now? Captor and Captive? There was certainly no future for them in *that*.

Was there any future for them at all?

18

"*Federales,*" Decker said. He looked at Fletcher and said, "Don't forget. You're a mute."

Fletcher nodded, his hand straying near his gun.

"And keep your damn hand away from your gun," Decker said. "There's four of them. Don't make a move unless I do. Understand?"

Fletcher nodded. That was good. Under stress he had already remembered not to speak.

Decker and Fletcher waited for the four *federales* to reach them. Decker noticed that the highest-ranking soldier was a sergeant. They were probably just a scouting party of some kind.

"Halt," the sergeant said, in Spanish, holding up his hand.

Since they had already stopped, they simply waited for the soldiers to reach them. When they did, the sergeant fronted them and the other three men surrounded them.

"What are you doing out here?" the sergeant asked.

Decker took a deep breath and said, "Just riding," in his best Spanish.

"Where?"

"No place in particular," Decker said. "Just riding."

"Are you bandits?"

Decker laughed and said, "Do we look like bandits?"

"Revolutionaries, then," the sergeant said, putting his hand on his gun.

"Are all strangers either bandits or revolutionaries?" Decker asked. "We are just two men riding."

"What is wrong with him?" the sergeant asked, jerking his head towards Fletcher. "Doesn't he speak?"

"No, he doesn't."

"Has he lost his tongue?"

Decker decided not to lie, because the sergeant might have checked.

"When he was small he saw his parents killed," Decker said. "He has not been able to speak since then."

The sergeant narrowed his eyes and asked, "Killed by who?"

Decker thought fast and said, "Bandits."

"Ah . . ." the sergeant said.

"Can we go, Sergeant?" Decker asked.

"Are you in a hurry to get somewhere?" the sergeant asked. He exchanged glances with his men, who were all grinning. Decker was starting to get a bad feeling in the pit of his stomach.

"I told you," Decker said, "we are not *going* anywhere. We are just riding."

"I see," the sergeant said. "Well then, you had better keep riding, eh?"

"Yes," Decker said, "all right. Whatever you say, Sergeant."

Decker started his horse, with Fletcher right next to him, on his right. They had ridden only a few feet when he heard the sound behind him that he had been expecting.

"Shit," he said, in English. He reached out and pushed Fletcher off his horse, then dove to his left, drawing his gun.

The soldier fired and missed. Decker hit the ground, holding his gun tightly so it wouldn't be jarred from his grip, then rolled over and fired. A soldier cried out and fell from his horse. He heard another shot, probably fired by Fletcher, and another soldier hit the ground.

Decker got to his knees and felt something tug at his sleeve. He paid it no mind and fired again, this time plugging the sergeant right in the chest. He drew a bead on the fourth soldier, but Fletcher fired and the man went off his horse backwards.

Decker and Fletcher both got to their feet and checked the four soldiers, who were all dead.

"How did you know?" Fletcher asked.

"You got to listen, kid," Decker said. "I heard the sound of hammers being cocked."

"You saved my life, Deck," Fletcher said. He rubbed his arm and added, "I think you broke my arm, but you saved my life."

As it turned out, his arm was just bruised, not broken. They ejected the spent rounds from their guns and replaced them with live ones.

"Better collect the horses," Decker said. "The shooting might have attracted attention."

"I think it already has," Fletcher said, pointing.

Decker looked where Fletcher was pointing and saw six riders.

"More soldiers?" Fletcher said.

"No," Decker said. "Worse."

"Bandits?"

"Unless I miss my guess," Decker said, "those are some of Fuljencio's men."

"Oh, great."

"Just stand easy," Decker said. "We just killed four *federales*. We've got that in our favor. And put your gun away."

Fletcher didn't answer, but when Decker looked at him he saw that the younger man had obeyed. He had also gone back into his mute act.

Good lad.

At that moment O'Grady and Jinx were crossing the Rio Grande. When they got to the other side, they stopped and looked around.

"So this is Mexico," Jinx said.

"This is it."

"Which way do we go?"

"We just keep riding south," O'Grady said. "We'll come to Malo soon enough."

"We better make it in time," Jinx said.

"For a million dollars," O'Grady said, "I think the general will allow us a little leeway, don't you?"

"A million dollars," she said, shaking her head. "You sure you don't have it on you?"

He looked at her and said, "Do I look like I have a million dollars on me?"

"I can't believe her father went along with this plan," Jinx said.

"He didn't."

"What? You mean—"

"He wanted to pay the ransom."

"So he *did* give you the money."

"But I don't have it on me," he lied. He *did* have the draft on him, but no money.

"What's gonna happen if she gets killed?" Jinx asked. "Then we'll have her father after us."

"I'm the only one her father knows about," he said. "If something happens, I'm the one he'll come after."

"Canyon," she said, "are you making all these decisions on your own?"

"Of course."

"Why?"

He looked at her and said, "Someone has to."

She stared at him and he could plainly see that she didn't believe him. That was all right. She had heard all he was going to tell her. If she didn't believe him, that was her business.

"We'd better keep moving," he said. "There are probably federal patrols all along the border. We don't want to run into one."

"No," Jinx said, "we don't want to do that."

"You will come with us," one of the soldiers said to Decker and Fletcher.

Actually, he was the only one who actually looked like a soldier. The other five men looked like farmers.

"Where?" Decker asked.

"To our camp," the man said. "The general will want to talk to you."

"About what?"

"You have killed four *federales*," the man said. "You have nothing to fear from us."

"I see."

"I *will* have to ask you for your guns, however," the soldier said.

"Of course," Decker said.

He took out his gun and handed it to one of the farmers, then looked at Fletcher, who did the same thing.

"And your rifles."

They handed over their rifles.

"When we get close to our camp we will have to blindfold you."

"Of course."

"Have no fear."

Easy for you to say, Decker thought, but he just

smiled at the soldier. Once they were blindfolded they could be shot and they'd never see it coming.

Have no fear.

"Stop," O'Grady said.

"What is it?"

"Up ahead."

Jinx looked ahead, then up and saw the buzzards circling.

"Oh, fine," she said.

"Let's go."

They rode on until they reached the spot that the buzzards were circling. There were four men lying on the ground, all wearing the uniforms of the *federales*.

O'Grady dismounted, handed Jinx his reins and checked all of them out.

"They're all dead."

Jinx looked around but didn't see anything.

"Dead about four or five hours, I'd say," he figured, walking around.

"Decker and Fletcher?" she asked.

"There's no way to tell," he said, crouched down, studying the ground, "but whoever did the shooting had company afterward." He stood up and pointed east. "They rode off that way with six others."

"What do you think, Canyon?"

He took back his reins and mounted up again.

"If it was Decker and Fletcher," he said, "they might have been taken by some of Fuljencio's soldiers."

"Why wouldn't they just kill them here?" she asked.

"Because *they* killed four soldiers," he said. "A revolutionary army can always use more men."

"You mean you think Decker and Fletcher are being recruited? But that's perfect!"

"Well, it puts them in Fuljencio's camp and not in Malo," he said. "That *could* work to our favor."

"And what do we do now?" she asked. "If we follow their trail, we'll find their camp. Or do we keep going to Malo?"

He looked at her and said, "Good question."

19

When the blindfolds were first applied both Decker and Fletcher experienced a moment of panic. Decker recovered quickly, figuring that there was nothing he could do about it, anyway. He just hoped that the kid wouldn't overreact. To his credit, he didn't.

When the blindfolds were removed the sun blinded both of them, and they raised their hands to block it out. It took several moments before they were able to see, and when they did they realized that *they* were the center of attention. They were surrounded by hostile-looking armed men.

The sergeant who had captured them said, "Get down from your horses. They will be seen to."

Decker and Fletcher dismounted and waited, exchanging a glance. They both realized that now that they were here and alive, this was a turn in their favor. They were actually *in* the rebel camp, where the girl was being held.

And there was only two of them against the whole camp.

"Wait here," the sergeant said.

Decker nodded and gave the man a weak smile. As the sergeant walked away the other men closed in on them, giving them barely enough room to breathe. Decker gave the kid what he hoped was a reassuring look. The kid looked as if he couldn't have spoken if he wanted to.

Decker knew how he felt.

When O'Grady and Jinx camped for the night, Jinx was very quiet.

"What's on your mind?" O'Grady asked.

She looked across the fire at him.

"If Decker and Fletcher are dead," she said, "we're riding into Malo cold."

"We have Preacher and Shea behind us," he reminded her.

"I'm a lot less confident if there's only four of us, O'Grady," she said.

"Then let's assume they're still alive," he said. "If they were going to kill them, they would have done it right there and then, and left their bodies next to the bodies of the *federales*."

"Maybe we should figure they're dead," Jinx said. "I mean, if we assume the worse we won't be surprised, right?"

"You could look at it that way, I suppose."

"All right, then, let's take it a step further," she said.

"All right," he said, pouring himself a cup of coffee and settling down with it, "you seem to want to talk about this. Go ahead."

"Decker and Fletcher are dead, and Fuljencio arrives to get his ransom payoff—without the girl."

"Then he doesn't get paid."

She stared at him.

"You didn't bring the money, anyway!"

"He doesn't know that."

"But he'll search you."

"So?"

"When he sees that you don't have the money—"

"He won't have to search me to see that," O'Grady said. "I can't have a million dollars hidden on me."

"All right," she said, "he searches our horses, and our rooms, he sees you don't have the money and that you never intended to pay him. So what does he do?"

"What?"

"He kills us."

"I don't think so."

"Why not?"

"Because then he'll never get paid."

"And how do you propose to pay him?"

"I don't."

"Then we're back to where we started," she said. "He'll kill us."

O'Grady shook his head.

"As long as he thinks there's a chance we hid the million, he'll keep us alive, and as long as we're alive there's a chance we can find the girl."

"I never realized what an optimist you are."

"And I never realized what a pessimist *you* are."

"I'm not," she said, "I'm trying to be realistic. Things have gone bad."

"You're assuming that because of four dead *federales*."

"That's right."

"I take that as a sign that things are going well," he said. "You said it yourself. If some of Fuljencio's men saw Decker and Fletcher kill the soldiers, they probably tried to recruit them. Decker is smart enough to take advantage of that."

"What if they realize that Decker is not what he's pretending to be."

O'Grady smiled.

"Decker's specialty is being what he's not. They'll never figure him out."

"You have a lot of faith in Decker."

"Hey," he said, "I have a lot of faith in all of you, that's why I recruited you. If you want to turn back, now's the time. I figure we'll hit Malo tomorrow."

"I'm not turning back," she said. "Don't worry about me. I'll do my part."

"I know you will."

"I'm just . . . you know, talking things out."

"Fine," he said, "no harm in that."

They drank coffee in silence after that and O'Grady had to wonder about Jinx the same way he had wondered about Shea. What was making her so nervous? Jinx wasn't yet thirty, but she had been on her own for a long time. Maybe it was finally starting to catch up to her.

He frowned, scolding himself for having judged all these people by his own performance. Just because he still felt confidence in his abilities didn't mean that they did, too.

"I'll take the first watch," she said.

"All right," he said. "Wake me in four hours."

He lay down, hoping that Anja Doyle's chances were still as good as he had originally thought them to be.

Decker and Fletcher, and O'Grady and Jinx in turn, had not been traveling at a fast pace. There was no need for that, since the ransom date was still three or four days away. That meant that even though Preacher and Shea were leading a pack horse, they were not being left farther behind. In fact, before they camped they *also* came upon the dead *federales*, only they had more options open to them.

"Whataya figure?" Shea asked. "O'Grady and Jinx?"

Preacher shrugged while he studied the ground.

"Could have been Decker and Fletcher."

"Whichever of the two it was, it's not too healthy for us to be stickin' around here."

"You've got that right," Preacher said. "Whoever shot these four had company right after. I make it six riders, and they all rode off together."

"Oh great," Shea said. "Somebody's been taken, but who? If it's O'Grady, we're out of business."

"Maybe," Preacher said.

"Whataya mean 'maybe'?" Shea asked. "He's the head honcho of this little operation. If he's out of action, we're all out of action."

"We'll just keep going and see what happens," Preacher said. "We'll assume that O'Grady is still in the play."

"You got a lot of faith in him," Shea said.

"You've worked with him before, Shea," Preacher said. "When he says he's going to do something, he generally does it."

"Yeah," Shea said, "yeah . . ."

"Let's move," Preacher said. "I want to put some space between us and this before we camp."

"Yeah," Shea said, looking down at the bodies and scowling.

"Hey," Preacher said, "we're still on schedule."

"Yeah," Shea said, "with the help of God, maybe."

Preacher gave Shea a long look and said, "Maybe you are not the heathen I thought you were."

Still scowling Shea said, "Don't bet on it."

Decker and Fletcher were kept waiting a long time. So long, in fact, that the sun was going down by the time the sergeant came back.

"Come," the man said, and they followed him.

They were relieved to get away from the press of the other revolutionaries. They were led to a tent and told to wait outside. The sergeant came out, and when he did he was followed by another man. He was tall, darkly handsome, about thirty-five, and seemed very much in authority.

"I am *Capitan* Roberto Velez Colon Salazar," he said. "And you?"

"Pepe Cardoza," Decker said, "this is my friend, Juan Bonilla."

Salazar looked at Fletcher hard, and then said to Decker, "I am told your friend does not speak."

"Alas, no, *Capitan*."

Salazar stared at Fletcher again, long enough to make the young man fidget, and then said, "Very well. I will speak to you, then. The sergeant tells me you and your mute friend killed four soldiers today."

"That is correct."

"Why?"

Decker allowed himself a small smile and said, "It seemed the thing to do at the time."

"The sergeant tells me your friend's parents were killed by bandits when he was very young."

"I lied about that," Decker said. "At the time I was not sure who your sergeant was. In fact, Juan's family was killed by *federales*."

"Ah," Salazar said, "then you had cause to hate the *federales*."

"Juan is my friend," Decker said.

"I am told you were very skillful in this."

"I have killed before," Decker said, "when I have had to. Juan is still young, and he learns very quickly."

"I see," Salazar said. "The sergeant feels that you might be worthy recruits for the revolution. You hate the *federales*, and you know how to fight. Men like that are always useful."

Decker executed a small bow and said, "It would

be our honor to serve General Fernando Maximilian Fuljencio."

"Perhaps," Salazar said. "The general would have to make that decision, himself."

"I understand."

"You will dine with us tonight," Salazar said. "You will have the freedom of the camp, but we will keep your guns. Do you have a problem with this?"

"No, Captain."

"Later, after dinner, the general will speak with you himself. If he approves, you will be recruited. If he does not . . ." The Captain ended his statement with a shrug. Decker knew what would happen if they were *not* approved.

"I understand, Captain."

"And your friend? Can you make him understand?"

"He is mute, Captain," Decker said, "but he is not deaf. He understands."

"Good," Salazar said, "very good. The sergeant will come and get you when the general is ready for your interview. Until then, you may wander about. Just do not go too far, eh?"

"We understand, Captain."

Salazar nodded, turned and went back into his tent.

Decker and Fletcher turned and saw many of the "soldiers" watching them.

"Do not worry, amigos," the sergeant said to them. "You have nothing to fear . . . yet."

When Jinx woke O'Grady, he said to her, "Okay, get some sleep."

"I'm not sleepy," she said. "I made a fresh pot of coffee."

He looked at her, sensed that she had something on her mind.

"You want to talk?"

She nodded.

"All right," he said, "let's get some of that coffee."

She poured two cups and handed him one.

"What's on your mind?"

"Canyon, I don't want you to think I've lost my nerve," she said. "It's important to me that you don't think that."

"Jinx," he said, "if you had lost your nerve you wouldn't be here, would you?"

"I wouldn't," she said, "if I was too stubborn to admit it, but that's not the point."

"All right," he said, "what is the point?"

"Lately, I've been . . . thinking about . . . things I never thought about before."

He decided to let her tell it in her own time.

"You know," she went on, "the kinds of thoughts women have?"

"Like marriage?"

"No," she said, shaking her head, "not even that. I mean, that's part of it, but . . . but I'm talking about the other part."

"Oh," he said, suddenly understanding. She looked at him, hoping that he did. "You mean babies?"

She looked relieved.

"Yes, yes," she said, "that's it, babies."

"So you want to have a baby," he said. "I think that's wonderful, Jinx."

"Not when you consider the kind of life I lead," she said. "I'm likely to get *killed* before I can ever have a baby."

"Lifestyles can be changed, Jinx."

"Can they?" she said. "Could you change? Could you settle down and be a father after the kind of life you've led?"

He opened his mouth, but no answer came out. Was she suggesting what he *thought* she was suggesting?

She saw his face and laughed.

"Oh, no," she said, "that's not what I'm suggesting, I'm just asking you to put yourself in my place. If you suddenly wanted a home and a family, could you change?"

He took a moment to think before answering.

"I don't know," he said, honestly. "I guess if I decided that it was what I really wanted, I could."

"Well then," she said, "maybe that's what I have to do. I've got to take the time to try and decide what I really want to do."

"It makes sense."

"Yes," she said, "that's what I'll do. When this is over, I'll take some time and think it over."

"Sounds like a good idea," he said. "What also sounds like a good idea is that you get some sleep now."

She looked at him and said, "Yes, you're right. All right, I'll turn in."

"I'll wake you at first light."

She nodded, stood up, wiped her hands clean on her thighs and walked to her bedroll.

O'Grady poured himself another cup of coffee and forcefully turned his thoughts away from *those* kinds of thoughts. A home and a family, despite what he had said to Jinx, were not for a man like him, and he chose not to think about them—at all!

20

The only thing available in the revolutionary camp for dinner was chicken. Chicken, it was explained to Decker, was the general's favorite food, and because of that they *all* had to eat it.

"I have eaten so much chicken," one soldier confided, "that I am about to sprout feathers."

It was difficult for Decker and Fletcher to find themselves alone so they could talk, but Fletcher found a use for his apparent muteness. Because he couldn't speak, men seemed to assume that meant he couldn't *hear*. Because of this they talked freely around him. That meant that once he and Decker *did* manage to find a moment alone, he had something to tell Decker.

"The girl is here," Fletcher told Decker.

"Keep your back to the others," Decker said. "We'll try and make it look like I'm talking, but you're not. Just keep nodding like a dummy."

"I'm no—oh, all right," Fletcher said, and nodded his head.

"What did you hear?"

"Those caves up there above us? That's where they're keepin' her."

Decker resisted looking up towards the caves.

"Well, this information will come in handy—that is, if they don't kill us first."

"What was all that Spanish about with that captain?" Fletcher asked. "I couldn't understand a word of it. I thought we were in."

Decker explained that they still had to be interviewed by the general himself before they were accepted.

"And if we're not accepted?" the younger man asked.

"Then I guess that'll mean we're dead."

"Hey," Fletcher said, "I ain't goin' down alone."

"That's an interesting remark, since we don't have any guns."

"I'll grab the closest one to me and take as many of the bastards with me as I can," Fletcher said. "You gonna be with me on that?"

Decker thought a moment, then sighed and said, "I guess we won't have much choice. Yeah, I'll be with you, but let's hope it doesn't come to that."

"I'll be hopin'," Fletcher said. "Now tell me, what's the business with all of this chicken . . . ?"

It was dark and there were campfires all over the camp by the time the sergeant came looking for them.

"It is time," the man told them.

Decker nodded and stood up, Fletcher with him. They both took deep breaths and followed the sergeant.

They were led to another, larger tent than earlier, and made to wait outside while the sergeant went in. Moments later he came out and beckoned them to enter.

Inside, the sight of the big brass bed surprised them, but even more surprising was General Fernando Maximilian Fuljencio. He was seated on the bed, naked to the waist, with a whole chicken in one hand and a woman in the other. The woman *was* naked, and had enormous breasts.

"I am told you killed four soldiers today," Fuljencio said, without preamble.

"That is true, *mi General*," Decker said, showing the proper amount of respect.

"And that you wish to join the revolution."

"Also true."

"If you are spies," Fuljencio said, "I will have you strung up by your tongues, and the flesh flayed from your bones. Is that understood?"

Decker swallowed—the con man in him thought it an appropriate touch—and said, "Yes, General."

Fuljencio stared at Fletcher, and Decker realized that Fletcher didn't realize what was being said, and so was not reacting at all to the conversation.

"Your young friend shows no fear," Fuljencio said, "I like that."

"He is a brave young man."

"And you?" Fuljencio asked, gesturing with the chicken. "Are you brave, also?"

"Brave enough to kill soldiers, *mi General*," Decker said.

"That is what I need," Fuljencio said, "brave men who can kill soldiers. Very well, you are members of my army. Your weapons will be returned to you—but beware. There will be eyes on you at all times until you have proven your worth."

"I understand, *mi General*."

"Now get out," Fuljencio said, "I have things to discuss with this fulsome young lady."

"Yes, *mi General*."

Decker nudged Fletcher, and the two men backed out of the tent.

"What was that all about?" Fletcher whispered urgently.

"We're in."

"But what was he talking about?"

"Believe me," Decker said, "you don't want to know."

Fletcher was about to say more when he was forced into silence by the approach of Captain Roberto Salazar. The captain was carrying their weapons.

"Here are your guns," Salazar said.

They accepted them, holstering the pistols and holding their rifles.

"When I give you the signal, you will be ready," Salazar said, looking around to make sure no one was near them to hear them.

"Uh, ready for what, Captain?" Decker asked, puzzled.

"Ready to take the girl and run," Salazar said.

Decker and Fletcher exchanged a quick glance. Even though Fletcher couldn't understand what Salazar was saying, he knew something was afoot.

"What girl?" Decker asked.

"Please," Salazar said, in English. "I am not a fool. You are no Mexican, and he is no mute. You are here to rescue the girl, no?"

"Captain—"

"Do not try to deny it," Salazar said. "I, too, want the girl to go free, so be ready to move when I tell you."

Decker still didn't know whether to admit it or not. This could have been a trick.

"You are only here and alive because I convinced the general that you *should* be alive," Salazar said. "I am your benefactor, and if you told the general this, he would kill *me*."

"I guess you're right," Decker said.

"So what do we do?" Fletcher asked.

"Tomorrow, the general will be sending some men

to Malo, ahead of time. I am to lead those men. The next day the general will go to Malo with the rest of the men. You will be among them. You and two other men will be assigned to watch the girl. I have arranged this."

"I see," Decker said.

"The first chance you get, take her and run for the border with her."

Decker thought a moment, then said, "We have some people in Malo, too, Captain."

"I think your job is to save the girl, no?" Salazar asked.

"Well . . . yes, but . . ."

"Then worry about her," Salazar said. "I will do what I can for the men you have in the town, but I can promise nothing. I am risking my life as it is."

"Why?" Decker asked. "Why are you risking your life for us?"

"Not for you," Salazar said. "For the girl. Keep her safe, or I will kill you myself!"

With that Salazar turned and walked away, leaving a stunned Decker and Fletcher behind him.

O'Grady and Jinx rode into Malo that night. It was a small, sleepy town of low adobe buildings. There was not a two-story structure anywhere.

"It's going to be kind of hard to find high ground for cover," Jinx said.

"Yeah."

They rode down the main street and didn't see any people.

"Is it deserted?" Jinx asked. "Did he pick a ghost town for the ransom payoff?"

"I don't think so," O'Grady said. He looked around and there *were* signs of life. The general store had some items out in front of the door. He could smell food cooking, and there was a trickle of smoke from the chimney of the cantina. "I think they just know that trouble is coming and they're staying off the street."

"That makes all of us," Jinx said, "only I don't guess we'll be staying off the streets, will we?"

"We'll be someplace we can *see* the streets. Come on."

They rode to the end of the street, where they found a livery that was unmanned. They took care of their horses themselves, and then left the livery with their rifles and saddlebags.

"Now what?" she asked.

"Now we find a place to wait."

"The cantina," she said. "We might as well eat and drink while we wait."

"Why not?" he said. "We've got a full day to wait, at least."

"I hope that's enough time for Preacher and Shea to catch up," she said. "And I hope Decker and Fletcher are all right."

"We'll know all of that pretty soon, Jinx," he said.

21

O'Grady and Jinx went to the cantina for dinner and were served tacos and tortillas along with some rice, and washed it down with cold beer. They were the only two people in the place.

"Excuse me," Jinx said to the man in Spanish.

"Senora?"

"Where is everyone?"

"Every-one?"

"All the people," she said. "Where are all the people?"

"They are home, *Senora*," the man said, folding his hands over his corpulent belly. "Bad things are going to happen very soon, and no one wants to be on the street when they do."

"Bad things?" she asked. "What sort of bad things?"

"Very bad things, *Senora*," the man said, shaking his head and wringing his hands.

As the man walked away Jinx looked at O'Grady and said, "Very bad things."

"I guess we know what bad things are going to happen," he said.

Jinx looked down at the food in her plate and then pushed it away.

"How can they call this food?" she asked. "I want a steak."

"You'll get one, when we get back to the United States. I'll buy you the biggest steak you ever saw."

"If we get out of this alive," Jinx said, "I'll be able to buy my own big steak."

She sipped her beer while O'Grady finished his food.

"What do we do now?" she asked.

"We could take turns watching the street," he said. "Or we could just both sit outside and watch the street together."

"I'll probably fall asleep," she said. "I could use a bath."

"Why don't you do that, then?" he suggested. "I'll take a chair and sit outside while you get a bath."

"You think there's a bath to be had in this town?"

"Check with the hotel clerk," O'Grady said. "He didn't seem to be doing much when we checked into the hotel. I'm sure he wouldn't mind drawing a bath for you. Just smile at him."

"I don't think he likes *gringas*," she said, "but I'll try."

They got up and O'Grady dropped some money on the table for the dinner. He went outside and found a straightbacked chair already there. He sat in it while Jinx stepped into the street and crossed over to the hotel.

It was getting dark, and O'Grady didn't think anything would be happening once the sun went down. Come tomorrow, though, he fully expected the general to send in some advance men to look the town over before they brought the girl in—*if* they brought the girl in. After all, since O'Grady never had any intention of paying the ransom, maybe the general never had any intention of giving them the girl.

It made sense.

* * *

151

It was pitch dark, with not much of a moon. Preacher was looking down at the few lights in the town.

"That Malo?" Shea asked.

"Unless we took a wrong turn someplace," Preacher said, "that's it."

"Don't look like much."

"I guess it isn't," Preacher said.

"Well, we gonna camp?"

"No," Preacher said, "we're going to take a ride around this town."

"For what?"

"To look for the best place."

"For what?"

"For you to do some damage with those toys of yours," Preacher said.

"I can do just fine from here."

"No," Preacher said, "there's got to be some places we can plant some. We won't know that unless we take a ride around."

"Can't we do that during the day?"

"During the day," Preacher said patiently, "we'd be seen. Come on, how long could it take to ride around this town?"

That made sense to Shea, so he said, "All right, let's do it."

When Jinx came back, she smelled clean and looked refreshed. She went into the cantina, came out with a chair and sat next to O'Grady.

"I wonder what Decker and Fletcher are doing right now?" she asked.

"I don't know," he said, "but I can tell you what Preacher and Shea are probably doing."

"What?"

"They're out there," O'Grady said, just jerking his

chin to the darkness that surrounded the town, "looking for a likely place to set up."

"I hope you're right," Jinx said. "What are you expecting to happen tomorrow, O'Grady?"

"I suspect the general will send some men into town to look it over."

"What will they do when they see us here?"

"Nothing," O'Grady said. "We're supposed to be here."

"*You're* supposed to be here," she reminded him.

"You're right," he said. "When we see them ride in, it might be better if you ducked out of sight."

"You mean make them think you're here alone."

"Right."

"Okay. That should give us some kind of an edge, right?"

"Right."

She paused a moment and then said, "Unless there's about thirty of them."

"Or so."

"And after tomorrow?"

"That's when I figure the general will put in his appearance."

"With or without the girl?"

"Exactly."

"I mean—"

"I know what you mean," O'Grady said. "It remains to be seen if he'll actually bring the girl or not."

"If he doesn't, we're in trouble."

"If he doesn't, it will mean he's just planning to kill us," O'Grady said. "I would say we'd be in trouble. I'd much rather he brings the girl."

"And then we'll try and get her free."

"Yes."

Jinx shook her head.

"How did I ever let you talk me into this?" she

asked. "I could be someplace right now, having a baby."

When it got late, O'Grady suggested they both go to sleep. Even if some of the general's men came into town in the night, they wouldn't try anything. He doubted that anything was going to be done until the general himself arrived. For one thing, the general wouldn't trust *anyone* with a million dollars.

O'Grady wondered if the general actually thought there really was going to be a million dollars?

Preacher and Shea made a cold camp that night. Just in case some of the general's men came early, they didn't want to give their location away with a fire. As the temperature went down, they wrapped themselves in blankets and took turns on watch.

"I don't know how I let myself get talked into this," Shea said. "I could be someplace with a warm, willing woman."

"Sinful thoughts," Preacher said.

"I know," Shea said, "they're the best kind."

Decker and Fletcher found themselves a space in camp and spread their blankets. Above them were the high rocks, where they had learned there were many caves.

"If we knew which cave she was in," Fletcher said, "we could go up and get her now."

"Look," Decker said, "now we've got the advantage of having the captain on our side, things don't look so bleak."

Fletcher looked at Decker and said, "We're right in the middle of a camp filled with revolutionaries, and you don't think things look bleak. I don't know how I ever let myself get talked into this."

"Didn't any of us need too much convincing," Decker said. "This just shows you what a man—or a woman—will do for money."

"Yeah, well," Fletcher said, "after this I'm gonna give a lot more thought to the things *I* do for money."

"Sure."

"I'm a young man, you know," he said. "I got a lot of life ahead of me."

"Right."

"I wanna make sure I get to live it."

"Sure," Decker said. "I don't blame you."

Fletcher looked at Decker and then said, "Shut up and go to sleep."

"Good advice. We got a long couple of days ahead of us."

Decker took a look up at the caves and momentarily entertained the thought of going up there and trying to find Anja Doyle, but she was sure to have a guard on her. Now that they had help from *inside* the camp, it would be silly to take the chance.

He wrapped himself in his blanket and tried to go to sleep, hoping that they *all* still had a lot of life ahead of them.

Jinx Quinones checked her weapons and then made sure they were both close at hand when she lay down on the bed. She knew she needed sleep, but she doubted she'd be able to get any. Being this close to the action never bothered her before, but then she had never been having these thoughts before . . . thoughts about what it meant to be a woman.

A baby. When had she first started thinking about having a baby, she wondered? She couldn't pinpoint it. Suddenly, the thought was just *there*, and there was nothing she could do to dispel it.

She closed her eyes, hoping that sleep would come, a deep, dreamless sleep . . . but she doubted it.

O'Grady looked out his window at the dark street outside. He knew that Jinx was in the room across from his, but decided not to go over there. Likewise, he was sure Jinx was determined not to come over to his room. Maybe, when this was all over, but not now, not right in the middle of what was essentially the firing line.

He thought briefly about Rufus Wheeler. Was he still in a hospital in Denver? Had he made his way back to Washington, D.C. yet? Had any headway been made in finding out who had shot him, and did it have anything to do with *this* situation, or was it totally unrelated? He didn't believe in coincidence, but he *hoped* it was unrelated, because if it wasn't then there was a possibility that General Fuljencio had some sort of contact in Washington, or Denver.

That was not a comforting thought.

O'Grady sat on his bed and checked his weapons. He had no doubt that, starting tomorrow, tension would be high, and they would be an eyelash away from having the entire situation blow up. He hoped for the sake of Anja Doyle they would be able to keep the lid on until it was *time* for the action to start.

Hours away, he thought. He felt that his senses were heightened at times like this, and he doubted that he'd get *any* sleep at all.

22

O'Grady was seated in front of the cantina with a cup of coffee when the riders came into town. There were easily a dozen of them, and they were all dressed alike, with sombreros, serapes and bandoleros. They *looked* like *bandidos*, but the man leading them was wearing a uniform and had sergeant's stripes.

This was General Fernando Maximilian Fuljencio's advance guard.

O'Grady stood his ground, even as the men rode by him and stared openly and curiously at him. He only hoped that Jinx wouldn't choose that precise moment to come out of the hotel.

The hotel.

What if Fuljencio's men took over the hotel for their stay? They'd find Jinx for sure. There was no way, though, that he could get up and get over there to warn her.

He hoped her instincts were as good as he remembered.

"Trouble," Shea said to Preacher.

Preacher, who had been sitting with his hat down over his eyes, stood up and looked down at the town.

"How many do you make?"

"Twelve."

"See a girl?"

"No."

"Okay," Preacher said. "The general probably sent them in ahead of time. All we have to do is sit and wait."

"What about O'Grady and Quinones?" Shea asked. "They're down there."

"They'll be smart enough to stay out of the way," Preacher said. "We wait."

The men he had come to think of as Fernando's Army had taken their horses to the livery. It was unavoidable that they'd see O'Grady and Jinx's horses. Jinx still hadn't put in an appearance. O'Grady hoped that she had looked out her window and got out of the hotel by a back exit. He hoped the hotel *had* a back exit.

The men split up. Four of them went to the hotel, and the other eight were heading for the cantina. He gave some thought to moving, but that would have just brought more attention to himself. He decided just to sit and wait.

The eight revolutionaries approached him and studied him curiously as they passed him and entered the cantina. The sergeant who had been with them was among the four men who went to the hotel.

O'Grady guessed that they were looking for him, but had been instructed not to approach him. If that was the case, then they were just going to be watching one another until the general showed up—with or without the girl.

It was likely to be a long wait—and if it wasn't long, it would *feel* long.

"Psst."

O'Grady turned and saw Jinx in the alley next to the cantina. He waved to show that he had seen her, and then she backed out of view, where she would stay.

O'Grady put the empty coffee cup on the ground next to him and decided against going into the cantina for another. If Fuljencio's men had been instructed to stay away from him, there was no point in his pushing it.

After about a half an hour, the twelve men came out again and starting moving around town, checking it out. The general wasn't about to ride in until he *knew* the town was secure.

O'Grady hoped Jinx had found a good place to hide.

Jinx was in the alley when the men started searching the town. Unfamiliar with the town, she was at a loss for a place to hide, but she had to find someplace.

"Hey!"

She turned at the sound of the voice and saw a woman in a doorway.

"Here," the woman said, waving, "*aqui*, come."

Jinx walked over to the back doorway. She could smell something cooking from inside.

"You are hiding from those men?" the woman asked. She was dark-haired, handsome, in her forties.

"Yes," Jinx said, "because—"

The woman cut her off with a wave of her hand.

"You do not have to tell me why," she said. "It is enough that you are hiding from them. Come, come inside. You will be safe here."

Jinx hesitated only a moment, then said, "Thank you," and stepped inside.

"Up."

Decker and Fletcher both looked up and saw a man wearing a soldier's coat with corporal's stripes on it standing over them.

"Come," the corporal said, "we are leaving."

Decker stood up and said, "I thought we weren't going until tomorrow."

"We are going now," the soldier said.

Decker was going to say something else when Fletcher nudged him from behind. Decker turned and saw two men coming down from the caves with a woman. She was disheveled and dirty, but he could see that she was not Mexican.

It had to be Anja Doyle.

Robert Salazar entered Fernando Fuljencio's tent, and caught the general in full uniform.

"Why has the schedule been moved up?" he asked. "I thought we were not taking the girl until tomorrow."

Fuljencio turned and looked at Salazar. There was no hint of the pig or buffoon in the man's face now. He was very serious.

"I have decided to go now," he said, spreading his arms. "Must there be another reason?"

"Fernando—"

"Get ready, Roberto," the general said. "The girl is being brought down now. We leave in ten minutes."

Salazar stared at Fuljencio for a few moments, then turned and left the tent.

Decker and Fletcher saw Salazar leave Fuljencio's tent.

"The captain doesn't look happy," Decker said.

Fletcher didn't reply, but his eyes said he wasn't happy, either.

O'Grady watched the men search the town, and then they congregated in front of the cantina, ignoring him. The sergeant spoke to one man, who went to the livery, got his horse, and rode out. The other men took up positions around the town, and the sergeant went into the cantina. He stopped at the door, looked down at the seated O'Grady for just a moment before going inside.

The town was secure.

O'Grady had a feeling that things were going to start happening fast.

Just two hours after the first twelve men arrived in town, Shea saw a larger group approaching.

"Now we really got trouble," Shea said to Preacher.

"Jesus," Preacher said, causing Shea to look at him in shock. "They moved up their timetable."

"Good thing we got here early, too, huh?" Shea asked.

"Shea," Preacher said, picking up his rifle, "take up the position we talked about last night. Don't do anything until either I fire, or O'Grady does. Got it?"

"Yeah, I got it," Shea said. "Good luck, Preacher."

"You, too."

The girl rode inside a circle of Fuljencio's men. Just outside the circle, Decker and Fletcher rode, trying to keep her within sight. She looked unhurt, and alert, and Decker knew she was trying not to show fear. She was a brave girl, and that would come in handy when the time came to make the break.

Up ahead of them Fuljencio rode at the head of the group, with Salazar riding next to him. Decker supposed they were supposed to be riding in some sort of column, but there was not enough discipline for that. The men were stretched out wide, and straggling behind. The men riding around the girl, though, they were trained, and they stayed close to her.

Decker saw Salazar look back several times, and

once he almost shrugged at the man. They would just have to wait for an opening.

They'd just have to wait.

O'Grady heard the horses before he saw them, and the men in the street heard them, also.

It was happening now.

From inside the store where she was hiding Jinx knew something was happening. She looked out the front window and saw everyone looking up the street.

"I have to go," she said.

"Do not go out there," the woman said. Inside the store was the women who had admitted her, along with a young boy of about twelve.

"Carlos, go out and see what is happening."

"*Si*, momma," he said.

The boy went out the front door, looked up the street, and then came back in.

"Lots of men, momma," he said, excitedly, "*lots* of men."

Jinx nodded and said, "Thank you, but I have to go out."

"Go out the back, then," the woman said. She unlocked the door and let Jinx out with a whispered, "*Vaya con dios.*"

23

Fuljencio stopped his men just outside of town.

"I will take twenty men into town with me," he said to Salazar. "Stay here with the girl. Do not bring her in unless I signal."

Salazar said, "Yes, General," even though he knew Fuljencio had no intention of *ever* giving such a signal.

They did not bring all of the men. Many were left behind in camp. There were eleven in town. The twelfth had ridden out to meet Fuljencio to tell him that the town was secure. Fuljencio was bringing twenty men into town with him, leaving a dozen outside with the girl. Among them were Decker, Fletcher, and Salazar.

That put the odds outside of town, by Decker's reckoning, at three to one.

He shuddered to think of what the odds in town were.

O'Grady saw Fuljencio riding in with about twenty men, and he did not see the girl. He could only assume that she was still outside of town, with a guard. He also didn't see Decker and Fletcher. If they were all right, he had to assume that they were also outside of town. That was good. They'd be able to snatch the girl when the action started.

As Fuljencio rode down the main street, the sergeant walked out to meet him. O'Grady saw the sergeant point his way without looking, and he took a deep breath and stood up.

Fuljencio left his men in the middle of the street and rode over to where O'Grady was standing.

"You are representing the rich American?" the general asked.

"That's right."

"Where is the money?"

"Where is the girl?"

"She is safe."

"I have to see her."

"I say what has to be done!" Fuljencio said. "I am in charge here!"

"You're not in charge of me," O'Grady said. "If you want to see the money, I have to see the girl."

Fuljencio sat his horse with his back straight and looked down at O'Grady critically.

"You did not bring the money, did you, *gringo*?"

"Did you bring the girl?"

"Of course I did," Fuljencio said. "I am a man of my word."

Looking the man right in the eye, O'Grady doubted that.

"I want my money," Fuljencio said, "or I will kill you where you stand."

"There will be no money, General," O'Grady said, "and I want the girl back . . . now."

Fuljencio gaped at O'Grady for a moment, then shook his head and laughed.

"*Amigo*, you are either a very brave man, or a very foolish one." He waved one arm and said, "Do you see how many men I have? And many more outside of town."

"All these men for me?" O'Grady asked. "And I

had heard tales of your courage, General. I guess those tales were not true."

Fuljencio's face darkened with rage.

"Which of these men have you chosen to kill me?" O'Grady asked. "Or will they all shoot me?"

Fuljencio angrily produced his revolver and said, "I will kill you myself."

O'Grady stared at the general, but in his mind he was saying, now, Preacher, now!

There was a shot, and an explosion, and suddenly men were falling, horses were crying out in panic, and guns were firing . . .

Preacher fired once. His shot struck a soldier, but he fired more as a signal to Shea than for effect. Shea, prepared for the signal, heaved a handful of dynamite from the roof they had chosen for him the night before, and it went off right in the center of the street, in the midst of Fuljencio's men.

From the other side of the street, Preacher began firing as quickly as he could.

From the alley, Jinx raised her rifle and began to fire.

O'Grady backed up, grabbed his rifle from where it was leaning against the wall, and began to fire.

When the first explosion went off, Decker drew his gun and began to fire. Fletcher followed suit. Fuljencio's men caught off-guard, had no chance to turn, locate the fire and return it.

Salazar, rather than kill his own men, drew his pistol and struck two of them, knocking them to the ground, thus saving their lives.

Anja Doyle, not sure what was happening, looked around her in confusion.

Decker rode up behind her and cut her hands loose.

"We're from America," he said. "We've come to take you back."

"Did my father send you?" she asked.

"Yes."

Salazar rode up to them and said, "Hurry, ride for the border."

"We've got people in town, Captain," Fletcher said.

The sound of more explosions and shooting came from town.

"I will ride into town and help."

"Why are you doing this?" Anja asked Salazar.

He looked at her and said, "You know why. In another life . . ." He stopped and looked at Decker, "Go now! Ride!"

"Fletcher," Decker said.

"What?"

"Take her and ride for the border."

"Where are you going?" Fletcher asked.

"Into town."

"I'm coming—"

"No!" Decker said. "The job was to get the girl to safety. Now do it! We'll meet you in Texas."

"Where?"

"Medallion, again," Decker said. "Now go!"

"Go," Salazar said to Anja.

They touched hands, the first time they had ever touched, and then he turned his horse and rode.

"And don't stop!" Decker said.

He turned his horse and rode after Salazar. Fletcher and Anja watched.

"How many more people?" she asked.

"Four others," he said.

"They'll all be killed."

"And us, too, if we don't go now."

"But—"

"Don't argue," Fletcher said. "Let's go!"

166

O'Grady ducked for cover behind a horse trough and looked around. He knew that Preacher and Shea were there, but he couldn't find them. That was good. If he couldn't find them, neither could Flujencio's men.

And what of Fuljencio? What had happened to him?

Fuljencio's men were running for cover now as more dynamite rained down on them.

O'Grady continued to fire, and reload, and fire. Eventually, they were going to have to make a break. Even with the explosives on their side, there were too many . . .

Jinx paused to reload, and realized that there were too many men for them to fight. She finished reloading, holstered her gun, and began to look around for horses.

As Decker and Salazar rode into town, the dynamite was doing less damage and simply causing confusion. Riderless horses were everywhere.

"Grab some horses and find your people!" Salazar said.

Decker saw the sense of that. Grab any horse and get the hell out of there. He holstered his gun and chased down one horse, then another. Now that he had two of them, all he had to do was locate two of his people.

Jinx ran into the middle of the street and leaped on a horse, then looked around and captured another. She felt something strike her shoulder, but didn't let it stop her. She located O'Grady and rode over with the second horse in tow.

"Canyon!" she shouted.

O'Grady saw her, and the horse. He ran for the horse, firing as he did, and mounted up.

"Go! Go!" he told her, tearing his horse's reins from her hands. .

They both turned their horses and rode south, in the direction of the livery. To ride north would have meant riding through the confusion. Besides, O'Grady had no intention of leaving without Cormac.

When they reached the livery he called out to her, "Keep going!" He dismounted and ran into the stable to find Cormac. Without bothering to saddle him, he leaped on his horse's back and rode him out of the barn.

Jinx was still there, lying on the ground.

Decker searched frantically for *someone* he recognized, and finally saw Preacher. The black-clad man was standing on a rooftop, firing down with his rifle. Decker rode over, pulling both horses behind him.

"Preacher!" he shouted.

Preacher looked down, saw Decker with the horses, and made his move. The rooftop was low, so he dropped to the ground, ran for one of the horses, and mounted up. Decker palmed his gun and gave him cover.

"Where's Shea?" Decker shouted.

"There!" Preacher said, pointing.

As he pointed Shea stood up, preparing to hurl another batch of dynamite. Instead, a bullet struck him and he dropped the explosives.

"No!" Decker said.

There was an explosion and Shea disappeared from view. The roof of the building he was on caved in, sending up great cloud of smoke and dust.

"He's done," Preacher shouted. "Let's get out of here."

"Where's O'Grady?"

"Taking care of himself," Preacher said. "Go!"

Fuljencio's men were firing, still not completely sure what they were firing at. Some of them were firing at each other. Some of them saw Preacher and Decker riding away and began to fire at them. Decker felt something in his side, but kept riding. He hoped O'Grady and Jinx would be able to get out.

O'Grady slid off of Cormac's back and rushed to Jinx. She was lying on her stomach, and there was a blood wound high on her back, on the right side.

"Jinx."

He turned her over and her eyes fluttered open.

"Get out," she said. "Leave me."

"I can't," he said. "You're going to have that baby, remember?"

"Sure," she said, "sure . . ."

O'Grady took her in his arms, stood up, turned and found himself facing General Fernando Fuljencio, who was pointing a gun at him.

"You tried to destroy my revolution," Fuljencio said.

"General, I have the money. It's in my pocket."

"You can't have a million dollars in your pocket."

"It's in the form of a draft, a bank draft. Take it."

"I cannot use your bank draft, *Senor*," Fuljencio said. "I need cash, and since you do not have that, I must say farewell."

O'Grady heard the horse and then suddenly there it was, bearing down on them. Fuljencio barely had time to look when the horse collided with him, sending him reeling to the ground.

The man astride the horse looked down at O'Grady.

"Go," Roberto Salazar said. "Get her on a horse and go. Quickly!"

O'Grady didn't ask any questions. He ran to Jinx's horse and placed her in the saddle, then mounted Cormac. He grabbed the reins of Jinx's horse and led it south, out of Malo.

Roberto Salazar dismounted and walked over to where Fernando Fuljencio lay, unconscious.

"The revolution will go on, old friend," he said, "but without the American million dollars." He looked up and shrugged. "We will do the best we can without it."

O'Grady circled Malo and found Decker and Preacher waiting north of town. Decker looked like he had taken a bullet in the side, but he was all right.

"Jinx?" Preacher said.

"She's hurt bad, but we'll have to put some distance between us and this town before we stop to do anything," O'Grady said.

Preacher dismounted anyway and pulled an extra shirt from his saddlebags. He crumpled it, tore it, pushed part of it under Jinx's shirt and tied the rest around her, tightly.

"That should slow the bleeding," he said, mounting up again.

"What about the girl?" O'Grady asked. "Did we get the girl?"

"Fletcher's gone with her," Decker said. "They're on their way to Texas."

O'Grady looked back at Malo, where confusion still reined, judging from the fact that there were still shots being fired.

"Shea?" he asked.

"Dead," Preacher said.

O'Grady shook his head.

"All right," he said, "we've got some riding to do, before they get their bearings back. Let's head for Texas."

Jinx looked at O'Grady and said, "I'm gonna have a baby."

The others looked at O'Grady, who shook his head and said, "Don't look at me."

RIDING THE WESTERN TRAIL

There's an epidemic with 27 million victims. And no visible symptoms.

It's an epidemic of people who can't read.

Believe it or not, 27 million Americans are functionally illiterate, about one adult in five.

The solution to this problem is you... when you join the fight against illiteracy. So call the Coalition for Literacy at toll-free **1-800-228-8813** and volunteer.

Volunteer Against Illiteracy. The only degree you need is a degree of caring.